Redstone's Valley
A novel by Ann Levingston Joiner

In the heart of the Texas Hill Country lies a gigantic pink granite batholith, stretching above the surrounding landscape, and visible for miles: the legendary Enchanted Rock, the geologic center of the state, and perhaps even of the contiguous United States. To the Tonkawa, the Comanche, and the Apache, as well as other native peoples, it was their Medicine Hill, their sacred Singing Rock. To the Spanish Conquistadores, it was La Roca Encantada. Today it is believed to be one of Earth's power points – a healing energetic vortex that many believe may contain portals leading into other worlds and times...

Ann Levingston Joiner

Chapter 1

The young woman heard the rumble and felt the shaking of the ground before she saw the mustangs. So did her horse. It raised its front hooves into the air as it whinnied in fear. When it did so, her thighs lost their grip on the pommels of her side saddle and she slid down the horse's back to the ground. Stunned by the fall, she helplessly watched the galloping herd come straight toward her.

She barely saw the man ride out of the herd. As he approached her, he slid sideways on his horse's bare back and lowered his arm in her direction. She pulled out of her haze enough to grab it, and the man straightened , pulling her up in front of him. The mustangs galloped around them and off across a tall ridge. The man watched them go.

"Well," he said, looking after them, "so much for a day's work." His soft southern voice had a New Orleans twist to it, which sounded familiar to the woman, since she had just returned to the Texas hills after five years attending school in that city. He turned to look at her and asked with blunt irritation, "You want to tell me who you are and what the hell you're doing on my land?"

Her anger pulled her back to reality. She pushed at the man and jumped nimbly to the ground, turned toward him, stood her full height, raised her head, and said, with a Spanish lilt in her voice, "I am Maria Isabela Antonia de Pineda y Soldana, and this, *señor*, is my father's land. Not yours."

The man swung his right leg over the horse's back and neck and bounded to the ground to stand beside her, bracing his hands on his hips. "I see," he said. Maria noticed that his light brown hair was long, that some strands of it glistened red-gold in the sunlight, that he was dressed in an open cotton shirt, buckskin moccasins and leggings. "And my name, *señorita*, is Daniel duBonviele He-Who-Rides-Two-Horses Thorne-Redstone and this is my land. Your father's line ended at the creek you crossed on the other side of this ridge." Without moving his hands from his hips, he pointed with his chin toward the ridge. "You're on the Double-R." He turned and walked toward her horse, which had stopped a few yards away after the herd had run off, and led it back to where she stood, confused a little by all that had happened in a matter of minutes.

"Double-R?"

"Redstone Ranch." He spoke the words slowly, as if talking to a child still learning to speak, and then bent toward her, cupping his hands to hold her booted foot. She automatically responded by accepting the gesture, and mounted her horse as gracefully as she could. As she settled her riding skirts, the man leapt quickly onto his own horse. With a hint of a twinkle growing in his eyes and the edge of a crinkly smile beginning on his face, he continued, in a Spanish more fluent than her English had been, "I am certain that Don Tomas is glad to have his daughter home, even if that school didn't quite finish her, as it was meant to do." He bowed slightly toward her. "Welcome back, Señorita Pineda, and please tell your father that I am still looking forward to having dinner at your *hacienda* tomorrow evening, but I must now begin rounding up my horses a second time." He nodded politely and rode away.

***

"He's insufferable!"

"*Hija*," Isabela admonished her daughter, "he is your father's *amigo*, his friend."

"He is still insufferable. Is he truly coming here for dinner tomorrow?"

"Your father invited him especially to meet you. He hopes you will become friends. Surely, you will not disappoint him. *El es su padre*, Maria."

"Then surely, Mama, my father would not want me to be insulted by this Texican *vaquero*."

"Daniel Redstone is no common cowboy, *hija*. His mother's relatives are highly respected merchants in New Orleans. Perhaps you heard of them while you were there. The Thorne family?"

"The name is familiar," Maria admitted, "but the man is still a boor. I do not see us becoming friendly, much less friends."

"Maria." The sharpness in her mother's voice contrasted with the concerned look in her eyes. "Do not tell your father of your feelings. *Comprende, hija*? I expect you to be considerate to our guest while he is here."

"Mama..."

"*Basta, hijita*. The conversation is finished."

The next evening Isabela stopped by Maria's room, concerned that her unpredictable daughter might still be intent on creating trouble for their guest. However, as she entered, she could not suppress a smile of delighted surprise.

"I thought you did not like this young man."

"I don't."

"*Verdad*? You seem to be going to a lot of trouble to look your best for someone you don't care to see."

"I intend," Maria responded with an arched eyebrow, "that before he leaves this evening, the *vaquero rustico* will know, once and for all, that, contrary to his opinion, I am quite well finished."

"*Terminado*? *Con que*?"

"Our dinner guest informed me yesterday, as his horses almost stampeded me to death, that my schooling in New Orleans did not quite finish me as it should have. Tonight he will see just how mistaken he was."

"Ah," Isabela smiled. "*Entiendo, hijita*. I understand now, perhaps better than you do yourself." She walked over to the bed where the red silk dinner gown lay waiting. "The dress is a good choice. You do have lovely shoulders. Leaving them bare will look quite elegant, *mas fino*."

"Mama, *por favor*!"

But Isabela had already left the room, her fears allayed.

Maria, however, was not so pleased as her mother. She was not looking forward to the dinner. She was determined to put the arrogant young man in his place. She looked once more in the mirror for reassurance before she called her *criada* to help her finish dressing. She stepped into the crinoline and fastened it to her waist as Lucia lifted the silk dress and placed it over her head, nestled its fullness into place and fastened the buttons that ran down the back. The dress did indeed show off her shoulders. "When this evening is over, Lucia," she said softly, "Mr. Daniel duBonviele He-who-rides-whatever Thorne-Redstone will know precisely who the hell I am."

Outside, she heard the sound of a horse pulling up to the main entrance to the *hacienda*. She picked up a book from the side table and sat very carefully on the edge of her chair as she smiled at Lucia and said in a conspiratorial whisper, "But he will have to wait a bit longer before he gets the opportunity.

Once she finally decided she should wait no longer, Maria started

5

down the hallway toward the *salon*. As she approached the room, she could hear the soft southern voice of the man who had treated her so rudely the day before. Even now, his voice had a grim tone.

"There is no way Governor Bell will not be reelected, Tomas." Even his laugh was rueful. "Being a Whig in Texas is about as useful as a thimble on a sinking ship."

She heard her father's commiserating laugh. "Thanks to the Germans, these hills seem the only sane place in the state. The plantation owners in the eastern counties make up less than a third of the people here, and yet, they control the legislature, and so, our laws." Maria heard his sigh as he added, "We must protect our land, Daniel. Our ties with the German settlers are almost as important as our continuing friendship."

Maria paused for a moment and pulled the bertha collar even lower on her shoulders and checked the voluminous skirt of her dress before she swept into the room.

"*Papacito querido, no mas hables de politico. Por favor, no se arresque de discordia este noche.*" After kissing her father's cheek as he stood to greet her, she turned, with a smile, toward the fireplace where Daniel was standing. Her voice caught, and she barely contained a gasp of surprise. She found herself looking at a man she might not have recognized were it not for his voice; he looked so little like the *vaquero* she had seen on the range only the day before.

Daniel's unruly locks had been pulled neatly into a queue at the back of his neck. The two-day growth of beard was now clean-shaven. The grey wool of his frock coat perfectly matched the grey of his brocade vest, as well as that of his eyes (or were they blue?), and his white linen shirt was held together at his neck with a silk cravat. Her only salvation was that he clearly looked as surprised as she.

"*No pasa nada, Señorita Pineda,*" he smiled as soon as he found his voice again. "*Su padre y yo estamos completamente de acuerda, especialmente sobre los politicos.*"

It was probably fortunate that Maria was so focused on Daniel's appearance that she did not notice the satisfied look that passed between her mother and father.

Don Tomas said to his daughter, "It is true. There will be no discord between us when Daniel and I speak of politics, daughter, for we are in accord in many ways, and even more so when it comes to our political leanings." He turned to include Daniel in his next statement. "But it is also true that we are now citizens of the United States, so perhaps we should be speaking English, is it not so?"

"Of course you are right, Papa. Especially since our guest is an Anglo. It was impolite of me to put you at a disadvantage, Mr. Redstone."

Don Tomas laughed loudly, then. "Hardly a disadvantage, daughter. Daniel is fluent in several languages, including Spanish and French."

"Growing up in the diverse cultures of New Orleans made it difficult not to be," Daniel smiled.

"And the two years apprenticeship aboard your family's merchant clipper added even more opportunities, I would think." The attraction Maria was reluctantly beginning to feel toward Daniel took a few steps backward. Why, she wondered, was her father trying so hard to impress her with this man?

Isabela intervened, and said sweetly, "Now that Maria has joined us, perhaps we should go to the dining room, before our dinner becomes cold."

"Of course, my dear. Daniel, Maria, please come this way."

"So, Mr. Redstone," Maria asked, once they were into their dinner, "were you able to recover all of your horses?"

"By nightfall, *Señorita*," Daniel's eyes had that now familiar crinkly twinkle. "Gentling them, however, may take a while longer than I had anticipated. They still seem a bit skittish. You gave them quite a shock."

She decided to ignore that last part. "Gentling or breaking?"

"I would never attempt to break a horse, *Señorita*, any more than I would a woman."

"Ah, but you would gentle a woman?"

"Maria, *por favor...*"

"But Mama, didn't Papa tell us we should speak English?"

"Please, daughter, show our guest that you can be a gentlewoman when you choose to do so."

"Don't worry, Doña Isabela." Daniel's twinkling eyes never left Maria's as he spoke to her mother. "To my thinking, having such spirit is admirable in a woman ...or a horse."

Don Tomas intervened. "You would see the difference between breaking and gentling, daughter, if you were to see Daniel in action. He has a true feeling for the animals."

"And for women?" Maria's eyes never strayed, either.

7

Daniel's face broke into a broad grin. He nodded appreciatively.

Don Tomas thought it a good time to change the subject. "So, you were saying earlier, Daniel, that you were certain Governor Bell will be re-elected. It is probably true. It is also very bad. His position on the land grants is not favorable. I am glad that you decided to study law once the school at Tulane opened."

"You have attended Tulane?"

"Since '47, when they added the law program. I finished last year."

"We were in New Orleans at the same time? I knew many of the students who went to Tulane."

"Thanks to my family connections, I was able to complete most of the work through correspondence. I was not at the university, or in the city, that often."

"And you will practice law now?"

"No, *Señorita*, but it was important to learn as much as I could, in order to protect our claims to this valley. The laws concerning land ownership are very complicated here. When I was born, thirty years ago, this land still belonged to Spain. By my first birthday, Mexico had gained her independence, and, as you know, the white newcomers, the Texicans, were inhabitants of Mexico. When I returned to this state from New Orleans, at sixteen, Texas had recently won its war for independence, and its citizens became Texians. Then, nine years later, just seven years ago, Texas was granted statehood, and now its people, as Texans, are citizens of the United States. So there are many factors at play, and many politicians who would use that complexity to their own ends."

"And this Governor Bell is one of those?"

"Indeed, and worse. Bell and his friends are a large part of the restlessness of the Penateka in this part of the state."

"Penateka, the Comanche?"

"Yes. They have a wise leader in Buffalo Hump, but most Texans refuse to see this, and are intent on running them out of the state entirely. Bell and others, like Jack Hays and his Texas Rangers, and like Samuel Maverick, want Texas to be all white - except for their slaves."

"And yet, my friend," Tomas injected, "you have to admit that Senor Maverick has been, shall I say, useful to you, in developing your holdings."

Maria noticed that the twinkle returned to Daniel's eyes with her father's comment.

8

"An unbranded calf is an unbranded calf, Tomas. If a rancher refuses to brand his herd, how is one to know if a cow is part of it or not?"

"So a maverick today isn't necessarily a part of Senor Maverick's herd, or even an animal. I have lately heard people refer to men who do not belong to any particular group as mavericks. Indeed, by that, one could even call you a maverick, my friend."

At that, Daniel's smile broke into a deep laugh. "God forbid," he chuckled, and then turned serious again. "Samuel Maverick was present at the Council House, and was part of the forces that fired on the Comanche chiefs there, who had come under a white flag to discuss terms for a treaty. The Penateka retaliated, of course, and were winning, until Bandera Pass."

"What happened at Bandera Pass, Daniel?" Isabel and Tomas looked at each other intently, noticing that their daughter had stopped referring to their guest as Mr. Redstone.

Daniel noticed it, too. His voice softened, and he spoke directly to Maria, very seriously. "It was the first time the Rangers used their Colt Revolvers. The Penateka are skilled warriors, but their arrows and lances were no match for pistols that could shoot five times without reloading. Peter Bell was there that day. I saw him."

"Then you were there, too."

"Daughter..."

"No, Tomas. This is something Maria must know."

"What is?"

"I was not there with the Rangers, Maria. I was there with my father and his band."

"Your father's band?"

"Yes, Maria. I am one-half Penateka Comanche. I was wounded that day, by a bullet from our esteemed governor's revolver. My father was killed in the battle."

"But you grew up in New Orleans."

Daniel could see that Maria was struggling with this news. "With my mother and her family. It is a complicated story. I did not know until I returned from my apprenticeship at sea, when I was sixteen."

"And you were sixteen when you returned to Texas."

"To find my father."

"And you found him."

"And lived with him for nine years, as a part of his band."

"And you fought the Texians."

9

"The Comanche are among the finest warriors of this country's indigenous people. They have had to be. For centuries, from the time of the Conquistadores, they have struggled to hold their land, and continue their way of life. It was a good way to live, as long as they were able to live it freely. They are warriors, yes, but they are also a very spiritual people."

"But you left."

"That way of life ceased to exist, especially after that day at Bandera Pass. Their bravery and skill could not withstand the superiority of the white man's weapons. They still fight, but only because they know no other way."

Maria said nothing for a moment. Tomas and Isabela watched in silence. "But," she then continued, "You must admit. They are a brutal people."

Daniel's voice remained low and gentle. "Is it not also brutal when 'civilized' men fire upon, and kill, those who come to them under a flag of peace, to clarify terms for a treaty? It is the white men who break the treaties, Maria. Only one has not been broken: the treaty signed five years ago by the Penateka chiefs and John Meusebach, in Fredericksburg, just south of here, and Fredericksburg is a German town."

Maria was silent again, for a while, and then said, "These men would drive us from our home, as well, even though our ancestors have lived here for over a hundred years." She leaned forward and placed her hand on Daniel's. "And you are a gentleman, and my father's friend. That is enough. I hope you will be my friend as well."

Daniel left soon after, and Maria went to find Lucia, to help her out of the silk dress. After she had changed into her nightclothes, she decided she wanted to talk to her parents, to find out more about this strange but attractive man who was her father's friend. As she walked back toward the *salon*, where he parents sat talking, she could not help but overhear their words. Perhaps it would have been better if they knew she was coming, but then, in the long run, perhaps it was another of those things she had to hear.

"So Daniel is in agreement?" she heard her mother say.

"Absolutely. It is by far the best way for us to complete our partnership, to protect our lands, and to protect Maria as well, especially since we have no son."

"It is too soon to tell Maria. It would be better if she had more

10

time to get to know Daniel as we do."

"I do not know how much time we can give her. She must know that she will have to marry, and sooner rather than later."

"And Daniel will be a good husband to her. I am certain of that - as good a husband as you are to me, *querido*."

Maria backed down the hallway to her room, but she did not go to bed for a long time. She just sat in her chair and stared into the darkness.

Chapter 2

Daniel singled out a roan mare and coaxed her into the smaller corral. Once it was just the two of them, he began to circle her. He spoke softly, uttering little chirping noises until she stood, quiet and curious, watching him closely. Slowly, he started moving closer to her until he could reach out his hand to touch her. The mare, listening and watching, did not move away. He continued moving in, finally running a hand along her back as he kept talking softly. Soon he was able to tie a soft halter around her muzzle. He started putting a bit of weight onto her back, then more, still speaking softly into her ear. He gradually added more and more of his weight onto her back, and then, slowly, he was astride her. The mare seemed a little uncomfortable, but did not move or attempt to buck him off. He pulled, just a little, on the halter, and she began to respond.

It was at that point that he sensed, more than saw, a horse and rider atop the near ridge just to the north of his home site. It did not take him long to see that it was Maria. She was not moving in his direction, just sitting aside her horse, watching. Focusing on the task before him, he continued to guide the mare gently around the small corral, until he reached the gate. The mare became nervous and backed away, but still did not attempt to dislodge her rider. He leaned forward and stroked her neck, still talking softly. They returned to the gate, and this time, as he lifted the latch, she walked him slowly outside. They began a slow climb toward the ridge where Maria and her horse stayed, still and waiting.

"Maria, he smiled, "I was planning to ride to the *hacienda* later this morning..."

"I know of your arrangement with my father," she snapped as he approached.

"Ride back to the corral with me."

"Why should I?"

"Because this little mare is not used to being ridden..."

"Unlike your horse, *Mr. Redstone*, I am not a piece of property to be bought, sold, and tamed."

"Of course you are not," Daniel replied softly. Please, come back to the corral with me."

Maria did not move, either forward or backward.

"We have much to talk about."

Her dark eyes regarded him coldly and she did not speak, but turned her horse and rode down the ridge toward the corral.

Daniel followed her, and on arriving back where he had started, he rode the mare back through the gate and dismounted before walking back toward Maria, latching the gate behind him. When he reached her, he lifted his arms, and helped her to dismount.

"So tell me, Mr. Redstone," she continued once safely on her feet, "What is a brood mare worth?"

"Before I answer your question, there is something I need to be certain you understand."

She tilted her head slightly, looking at him with expectation.

"Nothing will come of any agreement concerning you that your father and I have discussed unless you, too, want it to happen. It is true, as I hear you saying, that you are not a commodity. What you are, as I see you, is a beautiful, strong, and spirited young woman, whom I would like to get to know better, but only if you choose to allow it."

Maria was not to be disconcerted. She bit out her words. "Did you and my father not agree that I should become your wife?"

"We have discussed that possibility, yes."

"You...want to marry...me."

"Only if you...want it...as much as I."

"*Entiendo*, I understand. Now. If I am to be a part of this bargain, I need to know the terms. Just what is a wife worth to you? She looked toward the corral. "A horse or two, perhaps?"

Daniel looked at the young woman with growing admiration. She knew her position, but stood her ground, regardless. *Red is most definitely her color*, he thought to himself. The red wool of her short riding jacket was of a deeper shade than the silk dress from the evening before, and more sedate, trimmed with the same black wool as her full riding skirt. He knew that, for better or worse, he would have to put everything on the line now, without dragging it out any further, if he was to meet the challenge; and he knew, with growing intensity, just how much he wanted it to work. He gave her that little bit of a smile that he knew she had come to appreciate. "I gave a whole string of them for the last one."

"The last one..."

"My last - and first - wife." He tried very hard to look as innocent as he could manage.

"You already have a wife."

"Had."

"Had?"

"She stayed with Buffalo Hump and his band when I left to come here."

"You have a Comanche wife."

"While I lived with my father's band, but the Council granted her a divorce so that she could marry again after I left. She married a fine Penateka warrior, an old friend of mine."

"There is no way that my father could know this."

"He knows."

"Impossible, for he certainly knows that the Church does not recognize divorce. In their eyes, you are still married."

"In their eyes, I never was. The Church would not recognize a Comanche ceremony as a Christian marriage. As far as they are concerned, it never officially happened."

"Then, there were no children?"

Daniel allowed himself a sigh. At least, this was the last of it. "We had two sons."

"Had."

"They have a Penateka father now. That is best, for them, their mother, and for me. This is my world now. They would never be accepted here."

"Did you love her?"

"I had come to."

"And your sons?"

"Of course. But the Comanche way of life is over, as we discussed last night. I can survive here, but they would not."

"What makes you different?"

Daniel smiled ironically. "I have blue eyes."

Maria paused, then, before asking, "And how do you feel about her now?"

"I will always remember that I loved her, and the boys, and the life we had, but this is now." And now, this moment, Daniel sensed, was as important a moment as he had ever faced. He held both of his hands out to Maria. She waited before she took them. Daniel smiled an open smile then. He looked deeply into Maria's eyes. "I am strongly attracted to you." Then his eyes crinkled again. "I have been ever since you told me your name. And I sense, even now, that you return the attraction."

She didn't say no.

"I have learned that with commitment, it is possible for such attraction to grow into love. I look at Don Tomas and Doña Isabela, your parents, and I see two people who have come to love each other very much."

"Yes," she said in a whisper.

"And their marriage was arranged by their families."

"It was."

Daniel nodded. "May I shift the subject?"

"As you wish."

"This land," he turned a little and swept a hand across the landscape, "this valley, your father's *rancho*, these hills; is this not a special place?"

"It is home."

"More than home, Maria." He spoke with an intensity she had not heard from him before. "It is a sacred place. Do you not feel it?"

"I feel it," she almost whispered. "That is why the first thing I do when I come back after being away is to mount a horse and ride out into it."

"And into my herd of mustangs," he grinned.

Maria laughed with him, then, if a bit ruefully.

"I reacted badly," Daniel admitted. "It is one of the many things I hope you will forgive. But you do see," he insisted, continuing with his intense plea, "the importance of holding this sacred place, of not allowing the greed of some other owner to desecrate it?"

"*Yo lo creo.*"

"Your father and I are partners, Maria, because we love this land, and want to protect it. It is his hope, and mine, that you will join us, not as a possession to be bartered, but as an equal individual who shares our vision. *Cree lo que estoy diciendo*, Maria?"

Maria looked around her at the green hills and found her eyes focusing on the gigantic outcropping of red rock, the place the Comanche sometimes called Medicine Hill, sometimes The Singing Rock, the same place that the white settlers knew as the Enchanted Rock, and she felt, more than she actually saw, a shimmer of light seeming to emanate from it, sending a feeling of peace all through the valley and beyond, into the surrounding countryside. "*Asi lo creo*," she said in a bare whisper. She looked at Daniel, and said in a stronger voice, in English, "I will consider all that you have said."

It was now the time, Daniel realized. He released her hand and moved his own up toward her face, and cradling the back of her head he

15

leaned forward and - very gently - kissed her lips.

"Don't mind me."

Maria jumped backward, startled by the intruding voice.

Daniel merely looked a bit annoyed as he replied, "We won't," to the newcomer.

Maria looked toward the voice and saw a young man, dressed in the work clothes of a horse wrangler, leaning against the corral fence with an amused grin on his face. "You two just go on with what you were doing," he drawled. "I'll just wait here by the gate."

"I thought you couldn't make it before tomorrow morning." Obviously, the newcomer was someone Daniel knew.

"Town's quiet." The intruder replied. "Sheriff Martin said I might as well come on out today." Gesturing toward the corral, he asked, "That string ready?"

"Not quite."

"I can see you've been busy, Two Horses," the intruder nodded knowingly. That's a pretty new filly you've got there."

Maria's back went up sharply. "*Perdoneme.*"

"The roan mare, Maria."

That laugh in his eyes could be so annoying.

"It's him you'll have to pardon, miss." The intruder shifted his attention toward Maria. "He's lived in the wild, you see. Sometimes he forgets to be properly polite."

Daniel's eyes maintained that smile, and he looked directly at Maria when he said, with a slightly exaggerated formality, "Maria Isabela Antonia de Pineda y Soldana, may I present Deputy Sheriff Jake Holder of Fredericksburg," and added with a touch of irony, "a business partner I thought was my friend."

Maria wasn't ready to be cajoled by him just yet. "I see, Mr. Redstone," she replied in an even more formal tone than his had been. "I am curious to learn just how many partners you have."

"Oh, there's just me and Don Tomas, Señorita." Jake Holder assured her. "I'm assuming you are his daughter?"

"*Es verdad, Señor...*And just what is your business with my father's friend?"

"Mustangs, Señorita."

"Mustangs."

"Yeah, we round up a bunch; he gentles them, mostly, then I take them to town and sell them. Only I can't do that 'til they're ready to ride."

"Which they will be by tomorrow morning."

"Then I should leave you to your work, Mr. Redstone." Maria's voiced retained a cool formality, but became almost teasing when she added, "I have caused you too many delays already."

"I'm in no hurry." This came from Jake. "I'll just find me a hackamore while you two finish with whatever it was you were saying, or doing."

"Oh, we have finished, *señor*."

"The hackamore's in the tack room, Jake."

"Good, good." Jake headed toward the barn. "Señorita Pineda, please say 'Hello' to your father for me."

"I will do that, Deputy Holder."

As Jake entered the tack room, Maria turned her attention to Daniel. "Your...business...partner lives in Fredericksburg?"

"He has a wife and son there." Daniel explained. "The deputy's job gives him a steady income, and the horses take care of the extras."

"He is a close friend?"

"The closest." Daniel's voice turned serious. "I owe him my life. Literally."

"It sounds like an interesting story."

Daniel smiled gently, "I have many stories, Maria. I hope I will get the chance to tell you all of them before long." He helped her to mount.

As she nestled her skirts and prepared to ride away, she cautioned him, "I am still considering, Daniel." then softened a little, smiled herself, finally, and added, before she turned to ride away, "I like your friend."

Jake walked back from the tack room with the hackamore over his shoulder. "So," he asked, "when do I get Karin to press my good suit?"

"That's still an 'if,' not a 'when,' at least not yet." There was a slight irritation still lingering in his voice as he added, "You didn't exactly help, you know. Can't figure what was worse, your comments or your

17

timing."

"I don't know, Daniel," Jake drawled slowly, "It kind'a looked to me like you were doin' a pretty good job of persuadin'." The voice of the wrangler/lawman, whenever he was in a humorous mood, often took on more of the speech of his Kentucky roots.

Daniel opened the corral gate and the two men entered. Closing the gate behind them, he turned toward Jake and commented drily, "'Til you showed up. You might have whistled or something, friend."

"Think you'd have noticed? You were pretty engrossed in your, uh, conversation. I got the feeling that a future with this woman wouldn't be exactly painful for you, arrangement not withstandin'. She's definitely a fine looking woman." He started slipping the hackamore over the roan mare's nose and pulled it up behind her ears. The mare stiffened a little, but did not move away. He then started to rub her neck and back, taking time for her to get the feel of his presence.

"She's got more than looks, Jake." Daniel replied, shaking his head. He walked toward the corral fence and picked up a saddle blanket. "Quick wit," he added as he walked back toward Jake and the mare. His eyes twinkled a little, "Lots of spunk. She's her father's daughter, in a lot of ways. But," and he looked at Jake sharply and spoke emphatically, "the important thing is, we'd be joining the two properties. It will make for a lot more security for everybody, all things considered." The mare noticed the change in his voice and looked toward him. He brushed the blanket along her flank before carefully placing it on her back.

"Oh, I hear you, Two Horses," Jake put particular emphasis on the Comanche name. "And that's especially worrisome with my old Ranger acquaintance, Pete Bell, still sitting in the governor's chair."

"Not to mention Sam Maverick backing him in the legislature."

"Speaking of the Rangers," Jake added, "I heard from Sheriff Martin that Jack Hayes is the new sheriff of San Francisco County, out in California."

"California?" The mare started a little. The two men moved away from her slightly as they continued talking. "I wouldn't want to be the one to tell Buffalo Hump that Hayes has left Texas. Last time I saw the old chief, he was still smarting over the captain's claim that the Comanche were afraid to fight him at Singing Rock." He glanced in the direction of that gigantic red stone, off in the distance before he continued, "He made it pretty clear that he was planning to settle things up." Daniel shook his head. "The reason - the only reason - the Penateka let Jack Hayes alone once he started climbing that night, was because the Rock is sacred to The People, and attacking him while he was on it would have been a desecration. No way were they afraid of Jack Hayes." He was grimly silent for a moment before he added. "And you can bet that the man knew that."

"Sad thing is, that night is becoming another legend of Ranger Captain John 'Jack' Hayes, along with that bloodbath at Bandera Pass."

Daniel moved back toward the roan horse. "One thing you've got to remember about Bandera Pass, though, Jake. If you hadn't been riding with Hayes, Pete Bell, and even Kit Ackland that day, I wouldn't be here for us to complain about it."

"Maybe." Jake hesitated. "Daniel?"

"Uh-huh?" Daniel asked back. He seemed more concerned with the mare than with Jake's question.

"They say Kit Ackland went out there, too."

Daniel was silent for a time, focused on stroking the mare's back, before saying, in a flat voice, "It was my father's decision to attack your company that day. And from ambush."

"The pass was well inside the boundaries of the Comancheria." Jake pointed out. "It was his land; we were the invaders."

"And Sergeant Ackland was following his captain's orders, so he was doing his duty, and my father died honorably, in battle. It was the way it should have been."

"And you're okay with that?"

"Well," Daniel chuckled, flexing his shoulder as he remembered, "I can't say I voted for Peter Bell in the last election, any more than I will in this next one."

Jake laughed. "Me either, friend." After a minute he added, "As for Señorita Pineda, though, I was noticin' how business-like the two of you were actin'"

"Not everybody is as lucky as you and Karin, Jake; but I enjoy her company, and, as you said, she is fine to look at, so all in all, I can't say I'll mind too much if she comes around."

"Think she will?"

"Probably. She doesn't have that many options, when it comes right down to it." He was quiet for a minute. "She should have options. If I get the chance, I'll see to it that she has the opportunity to make her own decisions."

"I can see you will, Two Horses. In fact, I think I can see more than you do, where this Señorita Maria de Pineda y Soldana is concerned."

"Put that saddle on the mare, Jake."

Chapter 3

It was after finishing dinner and retiring to the *salon* at the *hacienda*, several weeks after Daniel's proposal, that Don Tomas and Doña Isabela quietly left the room as Daniel and Maria sat talking. Daniel noticed, but said nothing, focusing on Maria's words.

"It was at that little cafe next to the Plaza de Armas," she was saying, "near the corner of the Pontalba Apartments."

"Yes, I know the place. It was a favorite of my uncle's. They made a stew of boiled beef and vegetables."

"Just so; the food there was so simple, and yet the flavors were very rich. *Mi prima*, Imelda, and her mother, Tia Inez, and I spent many hours in *mi tia's cocina*, learning to get just that flavor."

"And did you?"

"I believe we came very close."

"Then I am almost hungry again, even after that large dinner. Maybe you will prepare it one day?"

Maria grew quiet.

"It looks like your parents have left us to ourselves."

"Yes. I wanted to speak to you...alone." She was quiet again.

"*Digame*, Maria," he said softly, "Tell me."

"I have a question about something you said the last time we were alone together - at the corral."

"*Pedirme lo que quieras*, Maria. Ask anything you wish."

"You told me that if we should...marry...that you would consider me a partner - *su compañera*, and you spoke of this place, this land, as sacred."

"This is true. On both counts."

"You spoke of the need we would have to keep the land safe. What specifically did you mean?"

"As to specifics, I can't say as much as you might wish to hear tonight. There are things that a man should only share with a wife." He took a sip of his brandy and looked into the fire before turning back to her, then leaned forward slightly and looked directly into her eyes. "My wife would be a - as you said - *compañera* - an equal partner with an equal voice in whatever choices and decisions would be made, especially about the home and family we would build together. For now, as to the sacredness of this land, and what that might mean, I must ask you to trust me."

Maria listened as intently as he spoke, returning his gaze as directly as he gave it. They had spent much time together during the past weeks, and she was coming to know more clearly just who this intriguing man was, as well as how he thought and behaved. "I trust you, Daniel," and after studying his eyes another moment, she nodded. "I would be pleased to be *su compañera*, Daniel, in all her aspects."

Daniel smiled, then, and set down the brandy glass before he leaned forward to kiss her again, this time, more lingeringly than at the corral. Then, without speaking, he reached into his pocket and pulled out a small ring, a gold band with one fiery, dark red stone. He lifted her left hand and placed it on her finger.

Maria's eyes could not help but sparkle then. She noted, "It seems you were confident of my answer, Daniel."

"Hopeful."

"It is a beautiful ring."

"To fit its wearer. Both the gold and the garnet are local, the gold from the river and the garnet from the rocks above it. It was made by a jeweler in San Antonio, who can easily adjust the size of it, if he needs to."

Maria shook her head at the last part. "A perfect fit," she whispered, still looking into his eyes, and, this time, it was she who leaned toward him.

The large blanket was spread out in the shade of one of the small oak trees that dotted the landscape between the creek and the large, pink granite land mass that the Spanish had named *La Roca Encantada*. In the mid-afternoon sun, the heat reflected a shimmering intensity, which did, indeed, make the rock seem enchanted. But the enchantment did not seem, to Maria, to include the two men who insisted on arguing like boys over matters that seemed to her to be inconsequential. She did feel the intensity of the discussion, though.

Jake lay on the blanket with his head in Karin's lap, reading the words of their fellow Texan, Sam Houston, from a folded newspaper: "There are but six men belonging to the Whig party in Texas, one of whom was a horse thief - another a black-leg - a third a land grabber, and the other three were mere tools and understrappers of the first three named..."

"Is that damned thing still around? It's a rehash from the last election," snapped Daniel, who lay leaning on his elbow next to Maria, who sat near a food basket, putting away some of the leftover ham that had been part of the sumptuous picnic.

"I don't know, Daniel," Jake drawled, "I can't help wonderin', which one are you, the horse thief or the land grabber."

"According to our current governor and his cohorts, they could both be either one of us."

"Except it clearly says 'Whig' Daniel." Jake pointed to the paper, "and we both know that I'm a Democrat."

"Who ought to know better. Karin," he added, turning to the pretty blonde, "haven't you been able to talk sense to him?"

"Daniel," Karin smiled, "what has a woman to do with politics?"

"You would, if this country had sense enough to allow you to vote."

"Well, we can agree on that one, anyway," Jake broke in. "Look, Daniel, before this country became a state, politics were simple: You supported Sam Houston or you didn't."

"And then Sam chose political clout over philosophy. That's why I could never be a politician. You have to sell your soul to get votes."

"And without votes, you don't get elected, and if you don't get elected, what good can you do?... Chase!" He broke off the conversation and called out to the little tow-headed boy who was running gleefully back and forth in the grass, oblivious to the heated discussions of his elders, "Come back closer to the blanket, son."

"Why, Papa?" the boy called back. He did slow down. He was old enough to understand that whatever his father told him to do had best be done, and quickly, but his three-year-old exhilaration was hard to contain sometimes.

"Because I ate too much to get up and come after you."

"At least it's an honest answer," laughed Daniel, instantly forgetting the familiar argument with his friend.

Chase walked, a bit slowly, back to the blanket, his head down and his steps trudging. "I want to go to the water."

"Not without us, *liebchen*," his mother admonished him firmly.

Chase collapsed onto the blanket, then, resting his chin on his fist.

"Tell you what," Daniel said to him. If it's okay with Mama and Papa, I'll take you to the creek for a few minutes."

"Papa, please?"

"Jake looked up toward his wife's face and asked her, "What do you think? Can we trust Uncle Dan to look after his godson for a few minutes?"

"Please, Mama?"

"On one condition," Karin said in mock seriousness. "When he brings you back, you must lie down and try to nap while he and Papa go for a walk."

"Nap?" "Walk?" "Walk?" The three males in the little group spoke simultaneously, causing both of the females to laugh heartily.

Karin looked down at her husband's head, still in her lap, "It will do you good after eating so much, and it will give Maria and me a chance to talk to each other instead of listening to your games. Isn't that part of what our picnic is about? A chance for us to get to know each other?"

"Well," Jake said with some resignation, as he rose to a sitting position, "if that's the case, I might as well cool off at the same time. "How about it son?" He ran his fingers through his hair and flexed his shoulders. "Is it all right with you if I come along?"

"Sure, Papa," Chase replied, and the three men were soon walking down toward the creek.

"Do you think it's safe to let the two of them go off together?"

Karin had to think a moment before answering, "Oh, the politics. It is just a game with them. They think the same things; they just look from different directions."

"*Es verdad*, Karin. You are right." Maria nodded, laughing, "Daniel and my father do it all the time, and they belong to the same party." She felt her hand and the ring on her finger that was still new and a little strange. "I am still getting used to all this."

"This?"

"This...*intimidad*...closeness?"

"Oh, I see, yes, it can be like that when love is still new."

"Daniel and I are not in love."

Karin's eyebrows rose slightly as she smiled.

"Oh, I admire him, and I find him very...attractive, but our marriage is to be...*un acuerdo*...an arrangement. It is necessary for Daniel and my father to secure their land holdings."

"Yes, this is what Daniel says to Jake and me, but we do not think so. We have known Daniel for some time now, Jake even longer than I, as he was best man at our wedding, and that was over four years ago. Perhaps Daniel doesn't know it yet, but we see and hear him, and we both believe that he loves you very much. And I don't know you well yet, Maria, but I see you looking at him sometimes, and I think maybe that you love him, too."

"Oh, I admire him, Karin. He is a man of honor; he will be fair with me, and with others, and that is what counts."

"And he is handsome, and wise, and able to provide for you?" Karin teased her new friend a little.

Maria held her left hand out a little, and studied the new ring on her finger. She spoke reflectively, "At first I was reconciled to what must be, then grateful, and now, the more I spend time with him, quite pleased. I must marry, of course. It is a good thing for both of us, and that is what matters."

"Ah, yes, I can see you are pleased. And when you are married, your pleasure will grow even more. You are not worried about that part, are you?"

"Worried?" Maria was puzzled at first, but then quickly understood. "Oh, no. In fact, as Daniel and I grow closer, I find myself wanting for us to be married very soon. And I am looking forward to having his children. I see little Chase, and want it even more." She looked toward the creek where the three boys were happily wading barefoot, with their trousers rolled to their knees. "He is such a darling child."

"Which one?" the women both laughed.

"I was speaking of little Chase."

"Ah, yes, Most of the time."

"But he is so smart, Karin. Such a wise little man, and he is like both of you. He looks so much like you, but his actions are so like Jake that it is funny to see them together. Daniel is very proud to be his godfather. He talks about him often."

"Daniel is good with children. He will be a good father."

"I hope we have several. Boys and girls, but mostly boys. My only brother died when he was very young. After that, Mama had a few miscarriages, and then nothing more. I know that my father misses my brother, and has worried about getting me settled into a proper marriage. I want to have sons for Daniel, so that he can be secure about the future."

"Jake told me that Daniel has spoken to you about his Comanche family."

"And of course he has told the two of you. That is good. You and I can speak freely, then. I don't like to speak of his personal life, especially the years he lived with his father. I am learning that he chooses to keeps those things to himself, with most people. Not because he is ashamed. It is only that few people would understand."

"Jake has told me that it took him some time to accept leaving his family. He saw them again, when the Fredericksburg treaty was being negotiated. He had a chance to talk with all of them, and was able to make his own peace."

"That treaty has been such a blessing for this valley. If only the others had been so fairly drawn."

Karin found herself looking at the ring on her own finger. "A special blessing for some of us. Jake and I met at the signing in Fredericksburg."

"Daniel has told me how much that meeting changed him. How he had been determined, after leaving the Rangers, to never be involved with enforcing the law again."

"And now he understands that it is his calling. He said Daniel pointed out to him that with the Rangers it was about making war; this work is about keeping the peace. It is a fine distinction, perhaps, but an important one."

"Is it hard for you? You must worry about him."

"Not really, Maria. For one thing, he is very good at the job, and he gets better the longer he works at it. I do not see any advantage to worrying. Isn't life a risk, for all of us? As women, this is something we know better than men, I think. We face it every time we give birth."

"Yes," Maria replied softly. "I do worry about that part of it sometimes."

"Oh, don't. The time of pain is so brief, compared to the joy of seeing your child in your arms. As soon as you hold him - or her, I am certain - the pain is quickly forgotten."

"You sound like Mama."

"So listen, and don't let it trouble you." Karin looked toward the creek and smiled again, "Life is a precious thing, to be savored, I think, for none of us have any guarantees that it will continue beyond tomorrow, no matter who we are or what we do."

Maria remembered what Daniel had told her about Karin. There was a sickness aboard the boat that brought the first settlers of

Fredericksburg to Texas from Germany. Many of them died, including Karin's parents, and all of her brothers and sisters. By the time she had arrived at the settlement, she was an orphan. She had reason to feel sorry for herself, but clearly, she did not. Maria thought carefully about the words her wise new friend had spoken, and said a little prayer for the circumstances that had brought their lives together. How good it will be, she thought, especially now, entering this new phase of her life, to have someone like Karin, another woman of her own age, someone gentle and kind, and who held such a strong and positive attitude toward life and the future. She took a deep breath, and vowed to let go of the faint misgivings that sometimes haunted her.

As little Chase slept soundly under the live oak with his mother and her new friend, Daniel and Jake hiked toward the singing rock. They found a crooked mesquite tree at the point where the creek rounded closest to the base of the granite hill and sat in the tree's ample shade. While they sat, Jake took a small tin flask from his pocket, opened it and took a sip before handing it to Daniel.

Daniel took it, and to answer his own curiosity, waved it briefly under his nose before he smiled and took a sip. "So," he asked, as he handed the flask back, "just what is it we are celebrating?"

"Just the fact that your bachelor days are numbered," Jake replied. "I thought you might need something to keep your courage up."

"Me? No, but drinking to the future seems like a pleasant idea. I have no qualms about these days coming to an end. I am thoroughly ready to take on marriage, especially to Maria. But I do need to take this chance to remind you of the duties of a best man. You may recall that I served those same duties for you, my friend, not too many years ago."

"I remember."

"Then you may recall that there were circumstances where I perhaps went above and beyond the line of duty?"

"I do. Thanks to you, Karin's German friends were foiled in their attempt to follow their traditions, and kidnap her on our wedding night."

"That kidnapping would have been a minor harassment compared to what is likely being planned at this very moment by my Louisiana cousins, who will be coming here for the event. And that is especially true since this particular custom is being adopted by too many Texans these days."

"A chivaree was not unknown in Kentucky, my friend. I take it that is the custom you are trying to avoid?"

"Jake, there is no way that I am going to allow Maria to be embarrassed by such raucous behavior. I have my own personal plans for our first night together, and those plans do not include you or anyone else besides the two of us. Do you understand, Best Man?"

"So, just what is it you are asking?"

"Two horses, saddled, bridled, and ready to ride, along with a pack horse that can travel fast, loaded down with provisions that will be prepared by me and Maria's *criada*, Lucia, hidden at the back entrance to the Pineda *hacienda*."

"That's it?"

"Along with a significant enough diversion so that Maria and I can slip away from the festivities without it being noticed until it is too late."

"Well, I guess I owe you that much, and I imagine that I can pull it off, but there is, still, the matter of the bed."

"The bed?"

"Our wedding bed, mine and Karin's. You managed to foul the kidnapping, but our so-called friends still managed to loosen the pegs holding the headboard to the bed frame."

"They loosened the headboard?"

"Another old German custom, I'm told."

"Of the bed you slept in on your wedding night?"

"That bed, yes."

"So, what happened?"

"Let's just say I thought for a few minutes that the earth really had moved."

Daniel tried unsuccessfully to muffle his laughter.

"Laugh away my friend. Remember, my debt to you does not go so far as that."

Daniel's eyes could not contain their merriment. "Oh, I can laugh, Jake. If there is one thing I am certain of, it is that there is no way that you or anyone else will be able to find this particular bride bed." He then gave in and stopped trying to hold back his laughter, and the two grown men howled in such merriment that they woke little Chase from his nap under the live oak tree with his mother and his soon to be Tante Maria.

28

"*Que hermosa mirar, mi prima.*"

"Thank you, *prima* Imelda, my cousin. The waist is a little tight."

"Tia Isabela was very slender when she was young, my mother says."

"Yes. She is still a handsome woman, but not so small as this dress. My laces are so tight I can barely breathe."

"You are not supposed to breathe, cousin," Imelda said with a smile, "You are only supposed to look radiant, to show you are in love."

"*Pero no estoy enamorado*, Imelda." she smiled back. "It is as I told you. Daniel and my father are partners, and our marriage will strengthen that."

"It seems you believe that is enough."

Maria smiled again, "*Pues* - well, you have met Daniel. Would you not think so?"

"What I think is that you do not know your feelings. I saw how you looked at him, how both of you look at each other."

"We have a strong respect for each other. This marriage will be a good thing. That is what is important." Maria changed the subject. "And speaking of important, you know what it is you must do, as the *fiesta* is drawing to a finish?"

Imelda sighed, and said, as if by rote, "I am to aid this Jake, Daniel's best man, in holding the attention of all of the guests, for a long enough time that you and your new *esposo* can slip away before the celebration is over."

"Exactly. *Es tan importante, mi prima* - more than my cousin, my maid of honor. It is your duty. *Comprende?*"

"*Comprendo.* Do not worry. It will be fun, doing such a romantic thing, especially for a bride who says she does not believe in love."

Chapter 4

They had been riding north at a good clip for hours, it seemed, Daniel leading their packhorse, and she, following closely behind. She was glad that he had insisted that she learn to ride astride, and in breeches instead of skirts. As long as the journey was taking, she felt much less tired and far more secure in her saddle.

Finally, they slowed, and came to a stop. Just ahead was a narrow river, and a series of short falls, spilling down over slabs of red-gold stone. Daniel motioned for her to continue following him, much more slowly now, and at first she thought they were riding directly into the falls, but as they approached closer, he led her through a gap between the wall of falling water and the rock, and soon, they were behind the falls, wading in a shallow grotto, with enough light coming through for her to see the red ground and walls of a cave beyond the pool. They rode onto the solid ground and stopped again. Daniel dismounted. He came to her with his arms uplifted to help her.

"We've lost them," he grinned. "We can afford to stop and rest now."

"How much farther?"

"Not far." He gestured toward a dark shadow where the rock wall of the cave seemed to disappear. "Through there," and he reassured her, "We'll soon be out on the other side."

"And then?"

"You will see...then." He smiled and gave her a light kiss.

"Well, then," she smiled back, "let's not waste any more time." She turned and remounted her horse on her own.

"You're ready? You're sure?"

"I'm not tired," she replied, "just eager to get to wherever it is that we are going."

Daniel walked to the wall of the cave and picked up a piece of wood, which he then lit to use as a torch. He remounted, and motioned for her to follow directly behind him. She took the reins of the packhorse and moved in closely. The narrow passage took several twists and turns, sometimes narrowing to the point that she wasn't sure the horses would fit through. At length they came to a wider, more open space, and Daniel dismounted, motioning for Maria to do the same. "From here, we will have to go on foot." He took the reins of the packhorse from her, and moved toward the other side of the small cave, into another passageway, this one with a sharp, rocky incline. After another turn or two, she started to notice a glimmer of light in the distance, which soon became a glow, and it was not long before they stepped out of the passage and into a small, misty valley. Even in the golden light of dusk, she could see the green of it. There were trees, taller than the scrubby oaks around her home, and, not too far away, a thin sliver of a waterfall emptied into a deep pool. Next to the pool stood a small stone house. The sun still shone enough to give the whole scene a golden shimmer. The air felt cool and pristine, and it was almost as though the surrounding hills and forest were singing.

"Oh, Daniel," she breathed. "It is as though we have entered another world!"

He looked at her a bit mysteriously as he smiled, "We have." Then he took her hand and walked her, along with the horses, toward the stables.

Daniel ceremoniously seated Maria on the ledge of the well, as he saw to the horses. He removed the bags from the back of the pack horse and placed them near the front door before her returned to where Maria sat, waiting curiously. He pulled her to her feet. "So, may I carry you across the threshold, *mi novia?*"

"*Por favor, mi novio. Tan pronto,*" she smiled mischievously.

Daniel opened the front door, picked her up, and carried her inside.

"Oh, Daniel," she said again as she took her first look around, "How beautiful it is. *Que perfecto.*"

He stood her on her feet, then, and reached outside for the bags; he placed one of them on a stone counter that separated what seemed to be a kitchen from the main room. There was a fireplace in the corner, with two large wood and leather couches in front of it, with a low wooden table between them. He took the other two bags to another room, probably a bedroom, off to the rear of the small house, then returned and removed his long frock coat. It was not until then that that Maria noticed he was still dressed in his wedding clothes. He had stayed in her parent's *salon* with the guests, giving her time to disappear and change. And then Jake and Imelda had managed to keep the guests occupied long enough for the two of them to make their escape and avoid the embarrassing customs of the wedding night. In their haste, Daniel had barely taken time to change into riding boots and loosen his cravat. Now he took it off entirely, along with the satin waistcoat, and dug the heel of each boot into a bootjack in the corner of the room. Once free of the formal accoutrements, he smiled broadly and spread his hands to show off his comfort. By then, Maria had removed her riding jacket, and sat on one of the couches. Daniel crossed over to her, lifted both her feet and swung them up to rest on the couch as he pulled her boots off and allowed her feet to stretch. He gave her a conspiratorial grin, saying, "Ahh. Free at last," as he bent toward her and gave her a light-hearted kiss, then straightened and picked up the bag from the stone counter and brought it to the low table. "Is anyone hungry?"

Maria did not ever remember seeing him quite so jovial. Not that he was often unpleasant, but there was usually a seriousness about him, like he carried a heavy responsibility that he couldn't quite let go. Here, though, in fact, from the time they entered the grotto back at the river, he had seemed to grow happier and more relaxed with every mile.

Sitting on the adjacent couch, he opened the bag and began bringing forth treasures, naming each as he placed it on the table. "Isabela's roasted beef with nopal cactus, fresh cheeses from the diary outside Fredericksburg, Lucia's famous fry bread, Karin's kolaches, both savory and sweet..." sounding like a maître'd at one of New Orleans' finest restaurants, "and, the best for last," with a flourish he produced two brown glazed bottles, "your favorite red wine from your father's cellar, from the cache which he acquired at the mission winery near El Paso last year."

Maria had caught his spirit by this time and clapped and laughed with delight. She had not realized just how hungry she was. "All of them my favorites, and I haven't eaten all day."

"At all?"

She had torn a small piece of fry bread and dipped it into the pot of meat. "I had to be certain that I could lace the corset tight enough for Mama's dress to fit." She ate eagerly, thoroughly enjoying every bite and every sip.

Daniel watched Maria as she heartily enjoyed the food in front of her. What need did she have of corsets, he thought - that simple shirt, tucked into a pair of her father's loose knickerbockers with her stockinged feet showing beneath them, her hair simply pulled straight back, and now with dark wisps of it hanging across her cheeks - *she is exquisite*, he thought, *and now she is my wife...*

He pulled himself up short, remembering her innocence. He did not want to rush this first night. He stood quickly, turned to walk toward the back of the room, standing at the archway, and looked quietly into the space beyond.

"Daniel?"

"Finish eating, Maria," he said softly, turning slightly to look back at her.

"I have." She said firmly, folding the cheeses and breads back into their napkins and into the basket, setting the wine glass aside and was rising to stand beside him when he came back to the low table. He picked up the basket, and took it into the kitchen, opened a small door in the stone wall, and motioned for her to come and look.

As she approached, she could feel the chill of a draft, and looking closer, could see a small clear stream running through a crevasse in the wall. Daniel placed the basket on a ledge next to the stream and closed the little door. It was like a very small springhouse, right there inside the kitchen. *"Que maravilloso!"* she whispered. "What a marvelous place this is."

"Only the beginning," Daniel smiled mysteriously. He led her back into the main room, and reached a hand to her cheek. She had come to expect the light kisses that had become common between them after she had agreed to their marriage. She lifted her lips toward his, and as he bent down and kissed her, this time, she found herself raising her arms and placing her hands around his neck, returning his kiss with a passion that surprised them both. Daniel took her in his arms and allowed himself to give in to the desires that he had been holding back from that first kiss at the corral. She surprised him even more as she lowered her hands to his chest and unfastened the buttons of his shirt. He pulled the tail of her blouse from her trousers and lifted it over her head, standing back a little, taking her body in, watching as she loosened the ribbon of her chemise. Then he slid its straps from her shoulders and drew her close to him until the tips of her bare breasts brushed against his chest. He felt them harden. She reached her hands to the thin ribbon that held his hair at the back of his neck and tugged it loose before reaching her arms back to the clasp holding her own hair and releasing it. When her hands moved toward the buttons that fastened his trousers, he laughed, and he picked her up and carried her into the bedroom.

33

Maria felt the morning sun on her face as it streamed in though the high window before she became fully awake. She opened her eyes slowly and looked at the man lying beside her, still sleeping soundly. She didn't want to wake him. Instead, she took the time to study his body, still bare from the night before. They had both fallen asleep immediately after their first lovemaking, the fatigue of the wedding day and their long ride finally catching up with them. She had been so intent on their passion that she hadn't really noticed the details of his body. She now saw that his muscled chest had a few scars. As she looked at the small round one near his shoulder, she remembered a comment he had made at that first dinner, that he still carried a bullet from Peter Bell's revolver. There were others, none very frightening, appearing to be left from minor knife wounds. She did not see them as disfiguring, just as an indication of the courage and strength of this man she could now truly call her husband. She shifted a little, feeling a slight soreness between her thighs, but thinking more of the profound sensations that had coursed through her whole body as they had shared the intimacy that her mother had assured her would be a pleasurable pain. Pleasure, she thought to herself, was a very mild word for it, and she could not hold back a delighted laugh. Daniel stirred then, and slowly opened his eyes. It seemed to take him a moment to remember where he was. Then, as he grew more awake, he smiled, and turned toward Maria, kissing her lightly.

"Good morning, wife." He greeted her, studying her face, "How do you feel this morning?"

She grinned back him and whispered mischievously, "Married," and bent her head toward his lips.

Chapter 5

After they had finished breakfast, Daniel turned to Maria and asked, "Do you remember, when we entered the valley, saying it was like we had entered another world?"

"And you said that we had. This house is what you meant."

"Not just the house, Maria. The valley itself, with the house, the pool, the spring that feeds it? If you try to reach them by going around, and not through the grotto, you won't find them. It is as though they don't exist."

"The grotto is the only way?"

"Not quite. There are others; I don't know how many, or where they all are, but our hills and our lands back home are all connected, somehow, to this...other world, as you called it." He took her hand, and led her to the back wall of the stone house, to the archway that had seemed to lead to a small niche. After they entered the space, Daniel put his hand to what had seemed to be the back wall, and when he did so, the wall moved sideways, exposing a landing and stairway, leading down and around. Daniel held her hand as they descended together. She could see a faint light coming up from the bottom, illuminating the way.

At the bottom, another archway opened out into a large room, or rather, a series of rooms, all opening one into the other. It was clearly a series of caves, but the stone walls, ceiling, and floors had all been cut and carved out in many places. It was difficult to tell at times, what was nature and what was construction.

There seemed to be a natural luminosity about the place, keeping it visible even though there was no discernible source for the light.

"Where are we?" Maria whispered. "Is this place real?"

"Is any place real?" Daniel asked her in return.

Maria looked at him quizzically.

He smiled again, and began to explain. "My Penateka father sent me on my first vision quest when I was seventeen. Before I left, his mother, my grandmother, spoke to me, as she had many times before. She was a wise woman, a Hopi woman my grandfather met during a long hunt into the far west. She had been my teacher, telling me the stories of the spirits and guides who could lead The People into the other worlds that are all around us, and of the doorways into their worlds, and how to find them. Such things, I suppose, are as close as a warrior comes to being religious, although religion isn't a very good word for... being in touch with the spirits and their medicine and powers." He continued, telling his new wife more even more about the way of his father's people. "The Comanche understand that all things have spirits, call them souls, perhaps. They are here, in the stones, all around us. The Penateka revere them; the Hopi have a strong sense of their world, and of their wisdom and knowledge. My grandmother shared what she knew with my father, and with me. It is through that wisdom that my quests, over time, brought me to the stone house above us." Daniel broke off and looked at Maria directly, holding her eyes with his. "That day we talked at the corral, you said that you also felt the strength of these hills."

"I remember," she whispered, "and here, in this place, it is even more intense."

Daniel nodded. "The hills of this area are especially sacred. The spirits are strong, the Comanche say. And they are strongest of all at the place they call the Singing Rock."

"Medicine Hill. I have heard it is haunted."

"Haunted? Perhaps, but the ghosts are not evil or malevolent. They will protect and speak to anyone who comes to them with a good heart. This is what my father and grandmother taught me." He looked at her even more closely and added, "Before I go any further, I must tell you: A Comanche's connection to the spirits, especially to his own guides, is a very personal thing, a secret between him and them, and to share those secrets can bring misfortune."

"But why, then, are you telling me?"

"Because a man's bond with his wife is also sacred. Once they are joined together, a warrior's wife must be entrusted, for the future of the family depends on their commitment to the secrets and each other."

"I am beginning to understand, *mi esposo*. Go on."

Daniel smiled. "Beginning is a good word, Maria, for what you see here is only a beginning to the secrets hidden in these hills and their caves and grottos." He stopped speaking, and reached a hand to her face, brushing a wisp of her dark hair that had fallen onto her cheek, and brushed it back behind her ear as he looked directly into her eyes. "Are you ready for a long walk, wife?"

"Lead the way," she smiled back, returning his gaze, "husband."

He took her hand and led her across the great room, through an archway, and down a narrow hall, to another stairway, which curved its way upward, and into a rough passageway, one that appeared to be a natural opening.   Daniel held her more closely as they continued, sometimes upward, sometimes down, and around narrow curves, and into spaces too small for them to walk side by side, so she followed him. The passageway was somewhat dark, but always, ahead of them was that luminescence she had noticed from the time they had crossed the opening back at the stone house.

At length, they stopped, and Daniel asked her, "Are you tired?"

"Not really," she said with some surprise. They had been going a long way, but she had no idea of how much time might have passed. "I feel something," she whispered the words, for it seemed the proper way to speak, somehow, in this place. "It is a new feeling, and strange, but in a good way. It is a peaceful feeling, and I feel strengthened by it."

Daniel nodded, "We are very close now," he replied softly, and they walked forward together, rounding a corner and into an open space, into a brightly lit cavern, an underground grotto, with a floor of red sand, and a pool of blue-green water glistening at one end.

Beyond the pool, the light grew more intense, and they entered another hallway, and the luminescence that had been guiding their way began to glow a strong red-gold. It led them into yet another room, where the light was even stronger, but not blinding or harsh. Maria soon saw its source, as Daniel stood behind her, his hands on her waist, turning her toward the light. They were standing in front of a glowing red stone, which was apparently the source of both the light, and of the feeling of peace and strength that had been growing in Maria as they had walked toward it.

"Redstone," was all she said.

They had stood, silently, for a while, taking in the warmth of that glowing red stone, before Daniel gestured beyond it, to an opening that emanated a green glow, coming from beyond it. As they walked in its direction, Maria started to hear a sound like rushing water, which grew louder as they entered another shaft, and then out into a green valley, with a rushing stream running across it. Maria looked up, expecting to see the sun, but all she could see, high above her head, was more of the red-gold rock, like that which had surrounded them from the time they had left the stone house.

Daniel walked to a curious-looking shrub, and picked some pieces of an unusual fruit, which he brought back to her. "Go ahead," he grinned, "It's good, I promise you, and I imagine you are hungry."

She hadn't realized it until he said it, but Maria was quite hungry, and thirsty, so she ate the fruit, which was as delicious as he had promised, then he went to the stream, made a cup from a large green leaf, and brought it back to her. She drank of the purest, clearest water she had ever tasted.

They had been sitting on the ground, close by the stream, when Daniel spoke to her again. "My main spirit guide, from the time of my first quest, has always been a deer. Whenever I am alone, lost, or in any kind of trouble, an old stag appears, and leads me to safety, and to running streams, like this one, with fresh water. When I listen carefully, the streams sing to me, as this one does now."

She looked at him, questioning.

He smiled at her and said, "Close your eyes."

She did so, and concentrated on the sound of the water spilling over the rocks, and soon, she could feel it, too. It was though the stream and the rocks were communing with her, whispering. She could not hear words, but she could feel a connection, and it gave her a sense of security that assured her that Daniel would always be a part of her, and she of him, and both of them a part of this peaceful, living, natural world.

Daniel touched her face, then, and she opened her eyes, and watched him as he spoke. "If we were to listen to the stream, and follow it," he pointed out its meandering path through the underground garden, and into the rocks on the side opposite where they sat, "it would lead us, eventually, to a cave that opens onto the top of the Singing Rock. We will not use it when we return home; it is a steep and twisted path, but I followed it from here, on my first quest. It led me in a full circle. I had begun my journey at the mesquite tree that grows from the highest point of the rock, and walked from there to the river. I was climbing the rocks beside a waterfall when I slipped and fell into the rushing white waters beneath the falls. I was pulled under the river, and into these caves. By the time I reached the stone, I was near death, but its light contains strong medicine, and has the power to heal. I spent several days in this garden, and when my strength returned, the spirit guides led me the rest of the way home."

Daniel continued softly. "I have told no one, except you, now, but after I returned to the band again, I listened, especially to my grandmother, who told stories of these underground cities, and of their caves filled with gold, silver, and stones of many colors. She told me many tales of other worlds, and magical places that held doorways into such worlds, like this one. After my father's death, when I left the Penateka, and brought my herds to the valley north of your father's *rancho* and *hacienda*, I remembered his warnings, and have listened to the words of some of the white men, both here in Texas and in Louisiana, and, I am sure, in other places as well - men of power and wealth and influence. I have become more and more convinced that the secrets of that red stone, which lies at the heart of this other, underground world, along with the knowledge of its powers, must be kept hidden, and have come to believe, as my grandmother told me, that it is my place, my destiny, and my responsibility, to guard it, in whatever way I can."

Maria had been listening, lost in every word he had spoken. For a few moments, she stayed quiet, still watching his face and reflecting on his story. After a while, she nodded. "Yes," she said firmly. "This is now our destiny, together, and the secrets must be kept."

And Daniel looked at his new wife, his new partner, and felt an immense gratitude, and silently thanked the spirit guides who had led him to this beautiful and courageous young woman. He reached toward her, cradled the back of her neck, and pulled her toward him.

They lay together in their bed in the back room of the stone house, with pillows at their backs, propped against the stone wall. Daniel took a small amulet from around his neck and handed it to Maria so that she could see it more closely. It was a familiar piece. He was wearing it the first day they met, and she would see it whenever he wore an open shirt. She had learned, since their wedding night, that he wore it always, even as he slept. As she held it, she could see that it was a red-gold stone, like a tiny piece of the larger one she had seen, hidden in the caves beneath them. It was intricately carved, in spite of being so small, not much more than an inch across. "It is a medicine wheel," he told her. "See how the center is a circle? The circle shows that all of life is interconnected. What happens to one of us happens to all. In my uncle's library in New Orleans,

I found and read a book of sermons by a 17th century churchman named John Donne. He spoke of this concept in one of the sermons. 'No man is an island,' he said. 'Each of us is part of the Continent, a part of the main.' and he explained it by saying, 'If so much as a clod were washed away, England would be the less.' This circle has the same meaning. See how it never ends?" He traced his finger around as Maria held the talisman in her hands, entranced by what her new husband was telling her. "It reminds us that life is eternal. And see, too, that this circle is divided into quarters? Four, my grandmother told me, is the number of totality, of the All, like the circle that holds them together - body, mind, emotion, and spirit, all working together, all of equal importance, held in balance by the constraints of that circle of wholeness."

He stroked his wife's hair as it lay across his shoulder and continued. "Our first obligation is to become a whole being, all parts of ourselves interrelated and working together." He continued to relate the teachings of his grandmother, remembering, almost word for word, as he went along. "It begins on the inside, within ourselves, and with knowing who we are, where we come from, and why we think and act as we do. It is a process that continues throughout our lives, each experience teaching us more, and helping us to understand why we are here. And as we come to know ourselves more completely, we can begin to know others, so that eventually, we can see their acts without judging them."

"First," Maria interjected, "take the plank from your own eye?"

Daniel nodded his approval. "Exactly, 'so we can see more clearly to help our brother.' That is a part of it, a very important part." He pointed again to the etched bit of stone, "Do you see how the four quarters of the circle are defined by a cross? When I was an apprentice seaman I traveled to many far places, learning about many different ways of life, and I found that the circle and the cross were often important symbols, even among so-called 'heathens,' who had never heard of our Christ."

He continued, in a slightly different vein, "When the medicine wheel is painted or woven, each quarter has its own color: white, black, yellow, and red. These colors represent the basic elements of our scientific world: air, water, earth, and fire. They also represent the four possible colors of human skin. When I was on the other side of the world, I saw many people whose skin was yellow, so it did not surprise me when my grandmother told me this was so."

He looked toward his wife again, and seeing that her face held a curious intensity, he continued, speaking softly, "Once we have come to know ourselves, we can begin to understand others, and let go of the need to judge them, and when we have found there is no reason to judge we can also see that there is no reason to feel shame, and so, no need to blame another."

He finished his explanation, summing up the symbolism of the wheel. "We are all on a journey - a quest - to find out why we are here, and what it is that we are here to do. That means we must be ever *mindful*, and aware of what is happening around us, and inside of us, so that we have the *courage* to take action," he pointed to each quarter of the circle etched into the stone talisman as he spoke, and he continued, "the *wisdom* to know which action, and the willingness to accept *responsibility* for the way we live and relate to others." He stroked Maria's hair again, and kissed her temple. "In this way, so I was taught, we live with honor."

They stopped along the creek for a quick lunch and a bit of rest. It had rained since they left the valley, and the creek was flowing. The water was running crystal clear, and the pink granite of its bed seemed to sparkle beneath the water. Little falls were formed as water spilled over the stones, and the stream meandered down the rise and across the valley toward its beginning at the base of that gigantic outcropping or red rock, clearly visible even though miles away.

"My father has always called it *La Roca Encantada*, the Enchanted Rock," Maria told Daniel. I have always felt that it was. Now I know for certain."

She sat with Daniel near the bank of the creek, under a live oak tree. Daniel's back rested against its trunk, with the back of Maria's head against his shoulder. He looked down at his new wife, smiling as he watched a gentle breeze pick up a few wisps of her hair, and tease them across her forehead. "Enchanted." he said softly. "And enchanting."

She turned her head so that their eyes met. "We should continue home soon." She looked back across their valley. "There is so much to do, now. I am eager to make the house our home."

The crinkle deepened around Daniel's eyes. "And just what do you plan on doing?"

"Not a lot. But I need to get to know the kitchen, to see if anything

41

should be added, and what supplies Lucia and I will need for cooking, and the windows could use some curtains."

"Curtains. I have to remember that it is no longer a bachelor's house. Do you think that Lucia will be comfortable with her quarters next to the kitchen?"

"Oh yes, I think so. I am so glad you offered to have her come with me. I have known her since we were little girls, and would have missed her."

Daniel took a few of the breeze-blown wisps of her hair and tucked them behind her ear. "You will need someone to help you with the house. I am glad she agreed to come."

"We will need to go into Fredericksburg as quickly as possible. Do you think Jake and Karin will mind if we stay with them for a night or two?"

"No, they won't mind. I will mind not having you to myself for as many as two nights, but it will be a while before we can manage a town house." He looked around him, silent for a bit, before saying, as much to himself as to her, "Fredericksburg is a long trip to make for supplies. It would be a good thing if we had some place closer."

"But what place would that be?"

"He looked around again, and said, as if the idea were somewhat new, "Why not this place?"

Maria looked around. They sat at a spot where the land leveled off into a low plateau, with the creek at one end, and a rise at the other. There was nothing in between except grass and a few cactus plants and the one little oak tree at their backs.

Daniel prompted her. "Do you recognize that rise ahead of us?"

She looked, puzzled, before she laughed, "I remember your mustangs trying to trample me."

"My apologies for that, but had they not unseated you then, we might not be sitting here together today."

"And I am glad that we are."

Daniel's musing grew more specific. "There is no stopping place for supplies between the Pedernales River at Fredericksburg and the Llano River to the north. It wouldn't need to be such a big place. A few buildings: a store or two; a barn and corral - for Jake and me to sell our horses without making so many trips to other towns." He looked around again, and his voice sounded more clear and determined. "A town, maybe; for a while, just a trading post. It could be a profitable and practical solution."

Maria took up his thinking. She looked at the stream beside them, glistening in the sun. "Sandy Creek?"

Daniel looked at her with even more appreciation. "Sandy Creek it should be," he smiled, as he pulled her chin toward his own.

Chapter 6

Stone sat at his new desk, trying to get adjusted to the shape of his chair as he acquainted himself with the office computer program. When the phone rang, he automatically picked it up. "Sheriff's Office. Deputy St... Shit." He took a few minutes to look more closely at the buttons. The phone rang a second time before he remembered which one he needed to push. He hit it and tried again. "Sheriff's Office. Dep..."

"Mack? Is that you?" The voice was a woman's, probably fairly young, with the slight drawl he was beginning to recognize as native to South Central Texas.

He rolled his eyes. "Deputy Stone," he finally got out, if somewhat abruptly.

"I need to speak to Sheriff White," the voice said with a touch or urgency and irritation.

"The sheriff isn't available." Stone replied bluntly. "State the reason for your call."

He heard the voice say back with equal bluntness, "I am reporting a theft...What did you say your name was?"

"Stone. What kind of theft, Miss?"

"Mrs. - Walters," he heard her say with more than a bit of annoyance, "Connie. Cattle, Deputy Stone, at least four head..."

Stone had turned the computer monitor so he could see it better, and put the phone on speaker so he could type. He interrupted her and spoke as he typed, "C-o-n-n-i-e?"

"K-h-a-n-i. How long have you been working for Mack?"

"Couple of days. You said cattle. What makes you think they've been stolen?"

"The fence has been cut. How long before I can talk to Mack?"

"He left for Austin this morning; won't be back until tomorrow. You want to talk to somebody, I'm it. How long ago did this happen?"

"A hand found the cuts on a routine line check. He called in to report it, and we know that several head were grazing in the area at last count..."

"Where is your location?"

There was a pause before the woman said, "You aren't from around here, are you Deputy Stone." It wasn't a question.

"Newark. Worked for NYPD. You want to give me that location

now?"

"Do you ride, Deputy?"

"Ride?"

"Can you ride a horse?"

"Not yet."

The woman sighed, "Then I'll have to meet you. Take Junction Road south as you leave town. Turn on FM 133 west and follow it about three miles. You'll come to a gate on your right, and an unmarked dirt road. We will meet there. Be prepared to walk."

"What...," but Stone realized he was listening to a dead line. He looked back at the buttons on the desk phone, thought a second, and punched a few of them.

"Sandy Creek City Hall. Rayjean."

"Jeannie, who the fuck is Khani Walters and how big a deal is four missing cows near a cut fence?"

"Oh, shit, Josh," the woman drawled, "Mack's in Austin all day isn't he?"

"That big, huh."

"Where'd she say it was?"

"Off Junction Road and 133, south of town."

"And you haven't started riding yet, have you."

"I've been on the job two days, Jeannie."

"I know, I know. Look, just take the Wrangler and be prepared to walk a few miles...and Josh?"

"Yeah?"

"Khani Walters is somebody around here, so try to be polite and charming, okay?"

"Too late, kid." He hung up the phone and looked through the drawers for the keys to the Jeep.

Khani Walters rode up to the gate next to the highway, pulled up, and dismounted. As she looked to the east, she saw an olive green Wrangler round the curve in the road and slow down. She unlocked the gate, swung it open, and waved. The Jeep pulled up and stopped. She knew without looking that the sign on the door said La Roca County

Sheriff's Department. The man who got out and started in her direction was tall, close to six feet, and muscular. He wore faded jeans over eastern-cut boots, a blue cotton shirt, and a well-worn brown leather jacket. His two-day-old growth of beard indicated he was one of those modern men who reserve shaving for special occasions. He was hatless. His light brown hair was relatively short, but a long shock of it fell over his forehead. He reached his hand up automatically to brush it back, and nodded. "Mrs. Walters?"

"Deputy Stone." She motioned toward the Wrangler and suggested, "You might want to pull the jeep up inside the fence and in a few yards. I can lock the gate to secure it. We have a way to walk from here." She spoke as matter-of-factly as she could. She had had enough of the man's sharpness over the phone. *NYPD*, she thought to herself. *What the hell was Mack thinking?* The deputy drove the Wrangler inside, parked it and walked over to where Khani Walters was standing. She held the reins of her horse; it walked along beside her. They walked in silence for a while. Finally she asked him, "What brought a New York City cop to the Texas Hill Country."

They walked a few more steps before he responded, "I wanted something quiet."

Was it a hint? Probably, but she was curious now. The man walking beside her would clearly be handsome, if he ever stopped scowling. "Well, you found it," she replied. "These hills are about as quiet as it gets." She wondered if she could coax him out of the scowl. "You won't have much more excitement than a few stolen cows, unless you count a couple of old lesbian ladies with a pot garden in their back yard. That's pot," she added, "the plant, not the container."

It worked, sort of. The man's eyes crinkled a little and he looked toward her with a hint of approval, if not a smile. She noticed that his eyes were grey. The shirt made them seem almost blue. "Mack warned me about them," he said, then added, "the ladies, not the cows."

She took his relaxed tone as a signal, and asked him, "How is the city doing after that attack?"

"Trying to get back to something like normal. It's not easy, with that big hole in the sky where the towers were, but New Yorkers are a tough bunch. They'll survive." He didn't say any more, but seemed to ease up a little.

She noticed he had begun to look at her more intently. In time, he spoke again. "Rayjean Simmons. The receptionist at City Hall?"

"I know her well."

"Cool lady. She said that you were somebody. I guess I'm curious. What does it mean to be somebody in... these hills?"

"Rayjean sometimes exaggerates. I guess she meant that my family has lived here a long time."

He looked at her closely again. "All of your family?"

"My father's family. My mother was Vietnamese. They met when he was there during the war. She died when I was still a baby. He brought me here when he left. It's the only home I can remember."

He nodded, "Khani with a 'K.'"

"Khan Yin. My father told me it meant 'precious stone that brings peace'." She felt a little embarrassed at being so open with this surly stranger, and shifted the conversation. "We're almost there. Beyond those rocks."

The terrain had been getting steeper as they walked. Pink granite rocks pushed out of the ground all around them and were growing larger and thicker. Ahead of them a group stood taller than the rest, seeming to form a circle. As they approached them, the ground leveled off, then dropped, and they could see a section of fence a few yards away.

Stone pulled out a notepad and started taking notes as they walked closer to the open gap, where the pointed ends of barbed wire coiled back. He looked closely at the area, squatting and studying the ground, the wire, and the fence posts. He ran his hand through his hair again as he stood and looked squarely at her. "So, what are we supposed to see here? You know these signs better than I do. The wire was clearly cut. Had to have been intentional." He looked toward the ground again, "Not many prints that I can see."

"It's hard ground. The prints are mostly from cattle hooves and shod horses."

"Shod?"

"Shoes. The horses wore horseshoes. That means someone was riding them, and driving the cattle through the opening. Range ponies wouldn't be shod."

Stone squatted again, looking more closely at the prints. "You said about four or five cows?"

"Steers. That's cattle that have been..."

"I got that one," he replied quickly, as he stood back up. He still seemed to be trying to be polite, almost friendly. "Sorry Mack wasn't here. He would probably have a better idea of what we are looking at than

I do."

"He might. Dan would for sure, if we knew where to find him."

"Dan?"

"Old Dan, most people call him. He's a hermit that lives somewhere back in the hills. No one knows just where, but if you want to learn more about reading sign and tracks, he would be the one to teach you. As for now, we've probably got all we can from what we can see. We might as well head back to the gate."

They had been walking a while, in silence. Stone seemed lost in his thoughts, and Khani sensed they were not completely pleasant ones. She decided that the man had reached the limit of his courtesy. They had almost reached the gate when the ringing sound of a cell phone came from the pocket of his jacket. He looked concerned, opened the phone and said, "What's up, Mike?" He listened a few seconds and asked, "Now?" He looked at his watch, puzzled, and spoke again, "Classes aren't supposed to end for another three hours..." Whoever Mike was talked a little longer as Stone looked more troubled. "Where is Chellie? Okay, look: Ask Mrs. Watkins if someone can stay there with you a while longer..."

Khani realized what must be happening, reached out a friendly arm toward him and said. "Early release."

Stone looked at her quizzically.

"Teachers' meeting." She saw he still looked puzzled. "Mrs. Watkins is the assistant principle at the elementary school. You have children there?"

"Two third graders."

"Let me have the phone."

Stone still just looked at her.

She motioned with her hand, and when he still looked hesitant, she took the phone and spoke into it. "Hey son, can you put Mrs. Watkins back on?...Mrs. Watkins? It's Khani Walters. I'm afraid I've pulled our new deputy out on a job. Would you mind calling Leticia and asking her to come to the school and get Mr. Stone's children and take them back to the Sunday house? Yes,... yes. Tell the Stone children that they have their father's permission to visit with the boys until he can get back..." Khani sent a questioning look at Stone. He shrugged and nodded, not knowing what else to do. "...and ask her to feed them, okay. Yes, I'll tell him,... yes. Thank you." She handed the phone back to him. "The letters to the parents went out last week. Someone should have thought to make sure your kids got the notices when they checked in yesterday, but it didn't happen. Mrs. Watkins said to tell you she is very sorry."

Stone nodded again but didn't say anything; he just looked uncomfortable.

It had to be difficult, a new job in a very different place, difficult for both children and parents, so she offered, "Mike and...Shelly?"

"Michelle. Michael and Michelle. They're twins."

"Do we need to get in touch with their mother? Is she working somewhere in town, or..."

The look Stone gave her then was one of such intense pain that she would later wonder why she hadn't sensed something unbearable had happened to him, something that caused him to be so distant and gruff. "Their mother is dead." Then he turned on his heel and walked silently toward the jeep.

Khani bit her lip, turned to the horse and deftly removed the saddle and bridle. She then gave a light slap to the horse's rump, and it trotted off. She knew it would head straight for home and dinner. She picked up the saddle and bridle and started toward the Wrangler. Stone came out of his grieved daze enough to take the saddle from her and put it in the open back. He reached for the bridle and dropped it in as well before he turned to her and gave a little shrug and half smile, which seemed as close as he could come, for the moment, to an apology. He opened the door for her to get in.

Maria awoke to the sun shining into the bedroom window. Daniel was still asleep beside her, his body close, giving support to her back, his hand lying protectively across her growing belly. The little one was especially active this morning, turning flips and telling her it was time to begin the day. She gently took Daniel's hand and moved it back as she tried to slip from the bed.

"Maria?"

"Go back to sleep, *querido*. Everything is fine."

Daniel turned, then, and was quickly asleep again.

Maria smiled. This *esposo* of hers did not like waking up in the morning, she had learned. She quietly changed into a loose wrapper and moccasins and went quietly outside and to the kitchen, where Lucia was already preparing breakfast. *"Es mas temprano, Lucia,* very early"

"Es por Diego."

Maria smiled. The *vaquero* had only recently come to work for Daniel. The herd was growing, and Jake was spending more of his time at home, with Karin's baby coming so soon. Lucia was taking especially good care of the young man, and Diego seemed to enjoy the attention. She reached for the coffeepot and an empty cup.

"Señora!"

"Don't worry, Lucia. It's for Daniel. He will be waking soon, and you know how it's always a good thing for his coffee to be ready when he does. Besides, it's been months now since the smell of it made me ill."

"You would probably not like the taste. Your body knows what is best for you and the *bebito*. You need to listen to it."

"Si, mi comadrona," Maria laughed. "It is good to have a midwife in the household, to give me orders, but don't worry, *esa bebita* is doing quite well. *She* woke me up this morning with her turning and stretching."

"If you are intent on a daughter, you are going to be disappointed, I think."

"I don't mind, either way, Lucia. I just like to tease you once in a while."

"Yes, well, you go on teasing, but remember, you are beginning your last three months, and you need to take care of yourself. That little one is going to grow more and more quickly, and become much stronger with its kicking and turning. You need to rest when you can."

"Now you sound like Daniel."

"So listen to him, and take him that coffee before it gets cold."

As Maria walked back to the main house, she thought about how this baby was changing her relationship with her *criada*, who was acting more and more like a mother, or at least, a slightly older sister. It was a good thing, since the *hacienda* was far enough away that Daniel and Lucia were both reluctant for her to make the trip too often. She liked the idea of having a woman around who knew so much about this business of having a baby.

Daniel walked out onto the veranda and down the steps, giving her a light kiss on her cheek as he took the cup. *"Gracias, querida."*

"A kiss and a smile so early? I shall have to tell Jake about this morning. He warned me, before we married, about what a grouch you would be."

"You look a lot better than Jake."

"Even now?"

"Especially now."

Daniel put an arm around Maria's waist as they climbed the steps back to the house. They were heading toward the sitting room when they saw a rider approaching from the south and riding fast. They walked quickly toward the front veranda.

"Who is it?" Maria asked

"Can't tell. Sure riding fast, though."

Daniel continued to watch the rider, and after a few minutes said, "Sheriff Martin."

"From Fredericksburg?"

Daniel was already down the front steps and walking toward the rider. Maria followed.

"Lou?" Daniel asked as the sheriff dismounted.

"Daniel. Maria." The sheriff nodded in their direction. "God in Hell, I am sorry to be the one to deliver this news, but we knew somebody had to come right away."

"Good God, what?"

"It's about Karin Holder. God, Daniel, they're gone."

"Gone? What do you mean?" Maria's voice registered shock and a sense of dread. "And what do you mean, 'They'?"

"Karin and the baby girl. She was stillborn, and Karin died just after."

They had been on the road for several minutes before Stone asked, "So, is Sandy Creek typical?"

"Of what?" Khani was still reluctant to say much more to this man until she knew him better.

"Texas towns. Everybody I've met so far has given me and my kids a lot more than I've deserved."

She relented a little. "Maybe you should go easier on yourself, Deputy Stone."

"Joshua. Josh."

"Okay Josh. Do you want to talk about anything or should I just shut up and let you drive."

"You've been great about Mike and Chellie. That's a big thing.

They...they miss their mother at least as much as I do, only they're just...they did nothing to deserve any of this." Talking about it was clearly hard for him.

Khani decided to keep things as casual as possible. "I just hope they won't mind eating Tex-Mex."

"Are you kidding? How do you think I convinced them this move was the right thing to do?" He even managed a small smile.

She laughed then, and decided to make an offer. "So how about you? Can you handle a couple of fajitas and a Shiner Bock?"

"Hey. Your Shiner Beer was the way I convinced myself." He relaxed even more. "I'm getting acquainted with fajitas. You offering chicken or beef?"

"Chicken??" Khani came back with mock horror, "you're investigating the theft of my *cattle* and you ask about *chicken?*"

Stone gave an exaggerated shrug.

"Tonight it's beef – Double-R organic Black Angus beef, but I admit we sometimes do chicken. Leticia can make just about anything taste good."

"Leticia. I remember. You asked Mrs. Watkins to let Leticia pick up the twins - and feed them...at a Sunday house?"

"Lots of ranchers keep a small house or cottage in the nearest town. It's an old custom that stuck. Before we had cars, a trip into town was a major undertaking, so a house there was almost a necessity, for buying supplies or going to church."

"Ah, a Sunday house."

"That's it."

"And Leticia?"

"Leticia is a distant cousin and an honor student at UTSC - that's University of Texas at Sandy Creek. She takes care of the boys after school and weekends. The Sunday house gives us a place to stay since the ranch is still a bit of a drive, and Leticia gets free room and board while she goes to school."

Stone nodded, "Okay, and I'm beginning to get what *somebody* means, but she deserves a bonus for her extra work today. What's the best way to handle that?"

Chapter 7

"'Episode One' again?"

"'Episode Two' is coming out in a few weeks. They have to be ready." The young, dark-haired woman looked away from tending the stove. "You must be Mike's and Chellie's dad. They're a couple of great kids."

"You'd be Leticia." Stone replied. "Thank you for looking after them." He handed her a folded bill.

"Oh, no, that's not..."

"Yes," Stone replied, firmly but with a kinder tone than he had used all day, "It is."

A quick glance was exchanged between Leticia and Khani, and the young woman smiled, "It really was a good thing for me. B. J. and Jack were so well behaved. They aren't used to having a pretty girl around."

Stone continued his effort to be what Rayjean had called polite and charming. "B. J. and Jack?"

"Bobby, Jr. and John David - "Jack." B. J. is nine and Jack is seven. Mike and Chellie fit right in. They've had a good time. That Chellie is a doll. She can quote Anakin Skywalker and Obi Wan Kenobi as well as any of the boys.

"'Episode One'," he shook his head. "Obi Wan is okay, but Anakin? I don't know what Lucas was thinking. The kid is just too cute to be Darth Vader in the making."

Khani noticed the charm with a bit of surprise. "I don't know Deputy Stone; I'll bet you weren't such a half-bad kid yourself."

"I guess I deserved that."

"A little. Leticia, can you get the new deputy a beer while I go change?" She smiled at Stone. "I'll be right back down."

Stone wasn't sure why she needed to change. She had kept her cool both physically and emotionally during the warm day outdoors. She looked at home in the jeans and plaid shirt, even though there was enough of an Asian-American look to her features for him to have guessed that she wasn't pure Texan. Her hair and eyes were brown, but with a touch of gold, and there was a hint of an oriental slant to her eyes. He realized it bothered him that he found her attractive. He took the dark beer that Leticia offered him, and tried to avoid sounding gruff. "Will Mr. Walters be coming soon?"

"Mr. Walters? Didn't Khani tell you? They're divorced. Bobby still lives in Houston. Khani moved back here with the kids to be closer to family, especially her father."

Stone realized it bothered him even more to be relieved. He took a sip on the cold beer and let it roll down his throat.

"I have to ride in to Fredericksburg."

"I'll get ready."

"You aren't going, Maria."

"The hell I'm not."

"It's too late for you to be riding..."

"Then hitch up the buggy while I change."

"Maria..."

"Good God, Daniel, do you honestly believe I can stay here?"

He looked at his determined wife and sighed. "I guess not."

"You damned well better guess not." She softened, and reached a hand to his cheek. "Get the team hitched. I won't be long."

As they pulled up in front of the Holder place, just outside Fredericksburg, people were already gathering. As Daniel and Maria looked around, they saw Karin's presence everywhere. Her gardens were blooming; you could feel her in the balanced arrangement of furniture on the wide front porch of the modest but well-cared for house; and her spirit seemed to be shining in the golden hue of the air around it all. They walked toward the porch as a red-haired and bearded man came down toward them. John Meusebach was the founder of this town of German immigrants, and a close friend of the deputy sheriff, and of that sheriff's close friends, Daniel and Maria Redstone. "Maria," Meusebach spoke to her directly, "it is so good you were able to come." He turned toward Daniel and took his hand. "He has been waiting for you both. He is in the back room. So far, he has not been able to come out and speak with the guests. Hopefully, you can give him some bit of comfort."

"Where is Chase," Maria wanted to know immediately.

"At a neighbors. He does not understand, of course." We thought it best to have him there for a while."

Maria's hands automatically went to her stomach. She said, firmly, "I will go to see about Chase. Daniel, you need some time alone with Jake."

Daniel nodded, gave her another kiss on her cheek, and started inside as John escorted Maria toward a nearby house.

The room was mostly dark. Daniel saw his friend staring out the only open window, toward the vegetable garden at the back of the main yard. "Jake?"

Jake didn't move or turn his head, but after a moment, he asked, "What do I do now, Daniel?"

"For the moment? Nothing. In time, you will need to look after your son."

Jake started a little. "Chase. Where is he?"

"At the neighbors. Maria is with him."

"Good, he likes Maria." Then he started again, "but, should she be here? You mustn't..."

"She's fine, Jake. I tried to get her to stay at home, but she was right. This is where she needs to be."

"Look after her, Daniel."

"I will. I do. Right now, I need to look after you. So, tell me, what can I do? What needs being done?" Daniel wanted to pull Jake out of his dazed grief. Doing something, anything, would help him to cope for now.

"Fraulein Martin is taking care of...them... right now. She and Karin are...*were*...close. John and Lou are looking after the rest."

"Okay," Daniel prompted, "So talk to me."

Jake's voice had a faraway sound, but after a brief silence, he did talk. "It worried her, a little. Me, going out and into town every day with a gun at my hip, not knowing what might come up, but I would reassure her that I knew my job, knew what I was doing. She never thought - we never thought - that it might be... God, Daniel. Karin was the image of goodness. She was..." He stopped talking, then, and continued to look out the window. After a bit, he spoke again. "Have you ever told Maria, Daniel?"

"Told her what, Jake."

"That you love her."

The question surprised him. "No, I don't think so...No, I guess not."

"Why?"

"It...just wasn't ever a part of our deal."

"But you do." He turned from the window, then, to look at his friend. "You do get that, don't you?"

"Yeah, Jake. I get it."

"Then do me a favor and tell her while you have time."

Daniel nodded. "You're right. I will."

"As often as you can." And then it started, finally, the tears that the strong man had been holding back began streaming down his cheeks.

Daniel moved toward his friend and gripped his shoulders, then held him tightly as the tears continued to fall.

They had been riding north from Fredericksburg for some hours when they reached the creek. Daniel pulled up the team and stopped, near the foot of the pink granite rock.

"Why are we stopping?"

"Because the horses need to rest, even if you are going to insist that you don't. For that matter, so do I." He climbed down from the seat and came around to Maria's side of the wagon and held up his arms.

She hesitated, looking around. "You know where we are."

"I know. It's our picnic spot - where we come with Jake and Karin."

"Came."

"I know that, too." He continued to hold up his arms.

Maria relented. She was tired from the long drive, and he was right. They all needed a rest, and here was the best water, and a good shade from the sun. She allowed him to help her to the ground. They walked toward the stand of live oaks. Maria could almost see Karin sitting beneath the largest tree, Jake lying along the ground in front of her, his head in her lap. The leaves over the trees were rustling in the light breeze, recalling the sounds of their laughter.

"There is something I must tell you, Maria, and it cannot wait any longer."

"Something else?" Maria's voice held a whisper of dread. They had been through so much during the last few days.

Daniel smiled at her, then, and ran his hand through her hair where the wind had caught it, and smoothed it back. *"Pobre querida,"* he said softly. "There has been enough bad news. It is time for something good to be said." He looked a little disturbed, then, before he added, "at least, I hope you see it as good."

"Well, tell me quickly then, *mi esposo,*" her voice lightly teasing.

Daniel was glad to hear that touch of lightness in her voice. He had been worrying about her, and their child, from the time they got the news about Karin and her baby. He pulled her toward him, and kissed her forehead, pushed her back a little to look into her eyes, and, realizing that he was more than a little afraid, he began.

"Do you remember the day we first met, farther north along this same creek?"

"Of course I do, and I remember the last time we were there as well, as we were returning from our honeymoon."

His eyes twinkled, just a little, then, as he asked her, "Did you have even the slightest idea, that first day, that the last one would ever be?"

"You know I didn't. I told my mother that you were completely insufferable. I wanted nothing to do with you."

"And yet, here we are. I hope I have never given you cause to regret our agreement, Maria."

"Regret? No, *mi esposo,* I have no regrets."

"Then, perhaps, you won't mind hearing what I have to tell you."

"*Digame,* Daniel. *Por favor,* please tell me."

The only way to do this was to do it, Daniel decided. He moved close to Maria and took her head in his hands and whispered to her, "*Te amo, querida.*" His eyes grew moist. "*Te amo mas de mi vida* - more than my life."

The emotions that she had held tightly in control over the last days slipped a little, as her tears rolled down her own cheeks. She responded even more softly, "*Y yo tu.*"

They said little else to each other the rest of the way home. The past few days had been so full of feelings they both needed time to digest them. It wasn't until that night, when she slipped into the bed beside him and they held each other closely, that she asked him, "How soon did you know?"

"That I loved you? It began the first day we met, but I was certain after you rode up to my corral and demanded to know how much you were worth. I could have - should have, told you then that you were priceless."

"Why didn't you?"

"I was afraid, I think, that I might frighten you away."

She laughed a little at that. "So much fear between us, over something so wonderful."

"I should have faced it sooner. So much of our time together wasted."

Maria moved his hands to her belly and laughed louder then. "I would not say the time was wasted, my love."

He laughed, too, then, and pulled her closer, into the sleeping position that they had begun to share from the time she had begun to show, spooned together, her back to his abdomen for support, and his hand protecting her and their child.

"Jake is going to need us," she said softly.

"Yes, and Chase."

"We will do what we can."

He held her more tightly. He thought she had gone to sleep.

"Daniel?"

"Yes?"

"There has been enough fear. I am not afraid, for me or for our child. Promise me you won't be."

Rather than lie to her, he kissed the back of her head, and said, as reassuringly as he could manage, "Sleep now, love."

After dinner, Stone went upstairs to check on the children. They all seemed to be getting along and contented, and Leticia was studying in her room down the hall from the TV loft, so he headed back down the stairs.

"Happy campers?"

"They're getting along great. Like they all knew each other a long time before today. Chellie's having a blast. Mike pretty much treats her like she's another guy, but B. J. and Jack both seem to know how to treat a lady. Must have learned that from their mother."

"I have to give their dad at least part credit for that. Bobby has always had the southern gentleman thing down pat."

"Have you been apart long?"

"A couple of years. Dad convinced me he needed for us to come back home. I'm glad we did, but I haven't really settled back in yet. Carl Jenkins, the editor of our local Gazette, keeps trying me to come to work for him, and I'm sure I will, but I still have some work to do at Dad's guest house before it's really comfortable for us, so I've put it off."

"A newspaper?"

"The only news in town. That's part of the problem. I wrote for a magazine in Houston. A newspaper requires a different kind of skill, like knowing who's new in town, especially if they work in law enforcement."

"We just got here a few days ago. It was kind of a quick decision for Mack and me both. You do seem a little less...inquisitive than most reporters I know, and that is a good thing. What magazine?"

"*The Texas Woman*. It's been around a while. It started back in the days of Betty Friedan and Gloria Steinham."

Stone raised an eyebrow.

"But we're a lot less militant these days. How about coffee?"

"Sounds good; can I help?"

"Why don't you go on out to the patio. The herb garden is already thriving, with the early rain and warm weather we had last month. I'll bring it out as soon as it's ready. Cream or sugar?"

"Black is good."

When Khani stepped out onto the patio with the coffee, she noticed that Stone was standing at the edge, leaning against the corner post and looking quietly out on the garden.

"You're right," he said softly as she handed him a mug of coffee. "That's some aroma. Back home, it would still be close to freezing."

"Give us another couple of weeks and the wildflowers should be blooming. Then you will see this Hill Country in its glory."

He smiled, but Khani could tell it was getting harder for him to play the charming guest. She took a seat in the wooden rocker and just let him be silent.

When he did speak, his voice was low and completely flat. "It was a pile-up on the Jersey Turnpike, just outside the George Washington Bridge." He took another sip of his coffee and turned more in her direction, but was looking more at the deck floor than at her. "A couple of hopped-up kids were trying to outrun a patrol car. Somebody on the road panicked, hit the brake and went into a skid. Next thing you knew, four other cars all got caught up in the mess and ran into each other. Erin's car was in the middle and got hit from two sides..." He stopped, tried to get his voice together, and then said, "The coroner said it was quick." And then he couldn't speak anymore.

Khani honored the silence for a while before she said, "I am so very sorry, Josh. How hard that must have been, must still be, for all of you."

"Yeah, it's hard, but that isn't all of the story." He stopped talking again.

Khani sat quietly. It seemed he needed to say something more, even though getting it out was clearly hard.

"Those kids? My partner and I had picked them up just a few hours earlier, walking the street, wasted. They were young, scared, and no priors, so we decided to let them off with just a warning. Told them to go home and sleep it off, and they said they would. I don't know where they got the car, but they must have driven it away just after we left." He shook his head. "Shit. If I had just done my job, what I was supposed to do... Mike and Chellie don't know about that yet. How in hell am I supposed to tell them?"

"You don't Josh. Not yet. Not while you're still carrying the responsibility for what happened."

"And how the fuck am I supposed to stop? I am responsible."

"As long as you see it that way, Josh, telling them would only put part of that responsibility on them. They're eight years old. Give yourself and them more time."

"People keep telling me time will help, but nobody can explain how, and I'm not all that sure I want it to."

"And any attempt I make right now will just seem frivolous. It would be frivolous. I've never been where you are. Hell, Bobby and I just...fizzled. I can tell you that I don't see you as the bad guy in this thing. All I can suggest is that you focus on Mike and Chellie, and accept our friendship."

The sound of children's cheers and clapping wafted down from the TV loft upstairs.

"There, you see? Once again, Anakin has stopped the droid army, Obi-Wan has killed Darth Maul, and Padme is back on her throne. Isn't that a good sign?"

"Except that it's a prequel, and we know things aren't going to end well for a very long time."

"Maybe, but just think, 'Episode Two' comes out this May."

"Oh, shit," Stone replied, but he laughed a little as he said it. He went inside and walked to the foot of the stairway and called up, "Hey, Mike; Chell. Get it together guys. It's time to go home."

Chapter 8

Stone settled his prisoner into the back seat of the van and locked the door. He went around to the driver's side, opened the door, got in, and buckled, trying to curb his annoyance. He knew that Mack was right. It had turned out that this bum he had picked up for vagrancy was wanted in Gillespie County, just to the south, on worse charges, so his extradition was necessary. So was the van necessary, even though Stone hated driving one. Like Mack had said, not only was the perp more secure, he would be less bothersome, separated from the front seat by a barred window and partition. Stone could focus on his first drive into Fredericksburg, the county seat of Gillespie County.

"An hour's drive at most," Mack had said. "Turn him in and spend the rest of the day on your own in Fredericksburg. I promise you, you won't be sorry."

So Stone shrugged and started the lumbering vehicle, and then eased it onto the street. "Take the main road south of town until you hit Ranch to Market 965 and turn right," Mack had told him. "Just follow it all the way into downtown."

Main road was a loose term. The two lanes meandered through hills and around curves bordered by grazing land broken by a few mesquite trees, some rocks, cactus plants, and low hills. Stone didn't know what he had expected, but when he reached the ranch to market road and turned onto it, he didn't find it much improved as highways go. It seemed only a slightly better paved version of the same rises, falls, and curves.

"What the f...," he found himself saying outloud. At first glimpse ahead, he thought he was seeing things, a trick of the eyes, brought on by the monotony of the landscape. He settled into another small draw before the road started climbing again. He rounded another curve, and blinked. There it was again. It disappeared again. He wasn't even sure what "it" was, the glimpses had been so brief. It appeared to be a hill, or maybe a small, low mountain, rising briefly out of the landscape, only it was different from the others, the green ones with their overgrowth of mesquite and skimpy live oaks. This one was more like a gigantic rock, or huge, monolithic, deep pink stone, looming just ahead of him. The road rose and twisted sharply and it was gone again. He still wondered if he had imagined it, it was so incongruous with the rest of the countryside. More rises and curves in the road. He thought he had seen the last of it. The road, now on something of a plateau, curved to the right, and right again, and then sharply swerved to the left, and there the damn thing was again, looming directly in front of him. The road grew straight, then, and led directly toward this great red stone beast, lying along the ground.

And then, something seemed to happen to Stone. He slowed the van down and approached more reverently, feeling almost as though he was approaching a sacred place. He wanted a better look at this thing which sprawled along, spreading out for over a mile along. The more he looked at this big, bald stone thing, the more it seemed to be singing to him, calling softly for him to come closer. Another rise and twist in the road and it was gone again, briefly, but soon back and even larger. It disappeared a few more times as the road resumed its twists and falls. Again, he wondered if his mind was playing tricks, only now he saw a sign, off to his right: "Entrance to Enchanted Rock State Park." Traffic slowed as cars ahead of him waited their turn to enter the park. Then, as he passed the entrance, he saw it up close, off to his right, a rise, or series of stone rises, of a salmon-pink shading into grey and again to almost red rock, rising above the surrounding countryside of grass, mesquite, and cactus. Once again he got the feeling that it was beckoning him to stop and come even closer. He shook away the feeling and continued his drive south toward the Gillespie County line and the little city of Fredericksburg, and its court house.

"You don't have to stay in Fredericksburg, Jake."

"Where else would we go?"

"Sandy Creek."

Jake shook his head, "I can't go back to wrangling horses, Daniel."

"I wasn't..."

"You were right, you know."

"About what?"

"I'm not a rancher, as much as I once thought I would be," he looked toward his friend with as much of a smile as he could muster, "I'm a lawman. I knew it from that day back in '47, when we were in Fredericksburg for Easter and the treaty celebration." His eye dimmed a little; the hint of a smile, gone. "That's when I met Karin, remember?"

"You were so set against putting that gun back on you were ready to walk away from her."

A little corner of Jake's smile came back, "...until you got me drunk and convinced me that it was my duty to stay and take on this job."

"I wasn't exactly sober myself that day, but as I remember, duty was your word. I think I said something more about it being your calling."

"Yeah, well whatever you call it, I made my peace with myself that day, along with the whole of Fredericksburg and the Penateka making theirs. I still remember what you said that convinced me: 'Laws are no better than the men who make them, and even then, everything depends on the people who are willing to enforce them. Who is right,' you asked me, 'who is wrong, and who gets to decide which is which?' Well, after that, I decided. I made my choice."

Daniel remembered as well, then. "Do you ever regret it?"

"Hell, no. I wouldn't have had Karin, or Chase."

"You still have Chase, Jake."

"He's what keeps me waking up every morning, forcing myself to get up and take care of my job."

"Karin was a part of this town...an important part...more than she gave herself credit for being. I still sense her presence here; it has to be stronger for you, but she and you daughter will always be a part of you, wherever you go."

"Like I said, Daniel, my job is here."

"What if you could do your job closer to the Double R?"

Jake just looked at Daniel with a get-on-with-it expression."

"Maria and I have been thinking that it would be a good thing if there were someplace a little closer than Fredericksburg for us to get supplies. I've corresponded with my uncle, William Thorne, and he agrees. He has been looking for a place to expand his shipping business into Texas from New Orleans."

"I thought you were dead set against getting back into your mother's family business."

"Was. I'm a..." He was about to say "married man," but decided it might sound insensitive, "...about to become a father, and a settlement nearer the ranch sounds better all the time. William has spoken to his contacts in Austin, and says they are ready to support the idea, even to establishing a new county, with a new town as its seat. We are looking at a piece of land along the creek, a few miles east of the Double R."

"Sandy Creek?"

"The town would be called Sandy Creek. How would you feel about being the new sheriff of La Roca County?"

"*La Roca*. The Rock. I like that." Jake walked to the window and looked out at the small fenced area at the side of his house, and the two headstones inside of it.

"That isn't where they are, Jake," Daniel told his friend, softly. "They are with you. They will be, wherever you go."

"So you're Joshua Stone." The olive drab uniform looked out of place on the dainty blonde sitting behind her desk in the clerk's office at the Gillespie County Jail.

Stone finished signing the release papers as he asked, "A reputation already? How did I mess up this time?"

"Mess up? Mack's new NYPD supercop?"

He looked quickly at the name plate on her desk before replying, "We're a long way from New York, Ms. Blake."

"Make it Betsy. Miss the big city life already?"

Stone actually laughed at that one. "That's not it, Betsy. From what I've seen so far, this is a good place; I just haven't learned my way around it yet. Until I do, I'm not sure how much help I am to Mack."

"Oh, you're doin' just fine. I got the scoop from the one who really knows what's going on in Sandy Creek"

"Friend of Rayjean Simmons, are you?

"Best buds forever."

"I was afraid of that." Stone thought it was time to change the subject. "Mack said I should take the day to get to know Fredericksburg. Any suggestions?"

"How much time you got?"

"Whole day, but I saw something on the way in I want to check out going back, so let's say the rest of the morning."

"Do you mind walking?"

"I lived in New York City, Betsy."

"Oh, yeah, well, there's a walking tour that covers most of the sites in town. If you drive the van over to the visitor center, you could park there. Just go inside and talk to Annie Sue at the desk. She'll give you a map and guide."

"Sounds good. What about food? What would you say is the best place to eat lunch?"

"My favorite place is the Auslander."

"Auslander?"

"Fredericksburg was settled by Germans, Deputy Stone. That's mostly what we eat here, German cooking."

"Just Stone, Betsy. German as in bratwurst?"

"Among other things, yes. Best bratwurst sandwich in town."

"Sounds like you know the menu."

"Want me to start with the appetizers or the beer and wine list?"

"If you're free for lunch, why don't you meet me there? My treat for the friendly welcome."

"I'm on an early schedule today, but if you head over to the center now, and get started, you should be through by eleven, and the restaurant will be open by then. If that isn't too early for you, you're on."

Stone found himself so caught up in the old world character of the Fredericksburg Historic District, he forgot to watch the time. When he checked, he could hardly believe it was nearly eleven, and he was several blocks from the restaurant where he was to meet Betsy. He had been walking for hours, but was more refreshed than tired. Every place he had stopped, he found friendly, helpful people. There was something about the air in this place. He had noticed it as soon as he walked out of the airport in San Antonio with the twins. Whatever it was, it had grown stronger that first day, the deeper he had driven into the hills. He was in one of the historical exhibits in the public library, learning more about the library building, which had been the county courthouse in an earlier time. It was an old Romanesque style building that was popular in Germany during the 1830's, and built here in 1883.

He left the building and hurried down Main Street, which ran through the center of town, a wide, four-lane thoroughfare with angled parking on both sides. The side where he was walking seemed like something out of the 19th century, a cross between Old Germany and the western frontier. Iron posts held up awnings and second-story balconies, and along the street, next to the curb, were wrought-iron benches flanked by large, half-barrel pots filled with brightly colored flowers, and even leafy vegetables.

He heard someone call his name and turned to see Betsy Blake walking up the street behind him. He stopped and waited.

"Looks like we have good timing. How was the tour?"

"Great, what I saw of it. I could spend a day apiece in some of these buildings. I have a thing for old architecture. Like that building up ahead, The Nimitz? The one that looks like the bow of an old ship?"

"Yes, Chester W. was one of our more famous natives."

"And his grandfather built the original part of the building in - what - 1852?"

"About then. That one, the library, and the Vereins-Kirche across the street from the library are probably some of the most photographed buildings in the state."

"The Vereins-Kirche is a reproduction."

"That's right. It looks the same, but the materials are different."

"I saw some pictures. It was originally fachwerk?"

"Yes, like many of the oldest homes here. Did you get to see any of them?"

"A couple. A real Old Europe look. Is this the restaurant?"

The Auschlander Biergarten had that same look of Old Europe, and once they were inside Betsy asked the hostess if there was an empty table on the patio as she sent a questioning look in Stone's direction as well.

He nodded his approval, and they were seated at a comfortable one with a red-checkered oilcloth cover.

The sandwich was as good as Betsy had promised, if not better. The murmur of soft-drawled voices around them was pleasant, and low enough that it did not keep them from talking. Betsy was easy to talk to.

"So, let me guess. That 'something' you saw on the way in was our local 'sacred place,' I'll bet."

"The sign said 'Enchanted Rock.'"

"That's it."

"Sacred?"

"To the native Americans who lived around here before they were forced into Oklahoma, definitely. But today, it's the New Age groups who say so, if you believe in that sort of thing."

"What sort of thing?"

"Oh, high energy spots, vortices, I think they call them. Some of these people even talk about portals."

"Portals?"

"Entry points, or so they say, to other times, or what they call parallel universes."

"No kidding?"

"A lot of people think so. I'm a skeptic, though. Too far out for me. But these people, sometimes in groups and sometimes just individuals, come here, some of them with special electronic equipment, even. They say it's like that place in Arizona."

"Sedona ?"

"That's it. Are you into that other-world stuff?"

"Heard of it; not into it."

"Well, I will say this, though. There is something about that place. It's a little freaky - in a good way."

"Good how?"

"I can't say exactly. It's just that being there makes you feel good. I can't explain it, but I've felt it, and so have most of the people who live around here. It has to do with why the native people called it sacred - that, and the lights."

"Lights?"

"Some evenings at dusk, or very early morning, they kind of shimmer over the top of it. It would be eerie, only the scientists have explained that part. I don't get the explanations. It's all over my head, but I take their word for it. It's made of a special kind of granite, and the rock itself is billions of years old - one of the oldest spots in the country, apparently. Oh, that, and it sings."

"Sings?"

"More like it groans and squeals, but the Tonkawa and the Comanche thought of it as singing. Can't say it would ever win a CMA, though."

"CMA?"

"Listen to the questions. You are a cop, aren't you? And a New York cop at that. CMA - Contry Music Awards."

"Got it."

Maria's head was caught in a swarm of pain, and Lucia's voice seemed distant and far away.

"You are doing fine, *señora*. Do not worry, it will soon be over."

Her mother was there as well, pressing a cool, damp cloth to her

68

forehead, and reassuring her that what Lucia was saying was true. It would soon be over.

Soon. She had been hearing that for a while now, and wondered how much longer it meant. For the moment, she was between the wracking contractions, and was trying to focus on Lucia's instructions about breathing. Lucia had assured her that everything was in order, that she and the baby were both healthy, and that she had nothing to fear. Still, she could not help but remember that, just a few months ago, her closest friend had died during this very process, along with her child. She had promised Daniel that she and this infant would be fine, that there was nothing to be afraid of. She had just not quite been able to convince herself. The pressure began again then, it was coming so quickly now, one wave after the other. This one was even stronger, the pain engulfing her to a greater degree than any before until she felt as though a part of her was lifting above her body, and at that point, for a moment, she felt free of it all, and then, from somewhere, seemingly a distance away, she heard a tiny wail that brought her back into her body. The pain was not so intense now, almost numbing, and she again heard Lucia's voice, *"Tiene un hijo, señora.* You have a son."

She came back to the present quickly then, hearing the cry growing stronger and more urgent. Lucia showed her the babe and the pain seemed to wither away. Yes, the baby was clearly a boy. After cleaning him, her mother moved him from her belly to her breast, and the little one quickly found it and gave its first suck. Maria watched, and knew she had never had such feelings of attachment as this. The new mother looked up at her own mother, and the two of them smiled together. Lucia massaged Maria's stomach, and soon, another wave of pain came over the nursing mother, but Lucia reassured her that all was well.

"Es solo la placenta, señora. The afterbirth. That, too, was expelled quickly, and the cord that connected Maria to her infant was cut. They were now, for the first time since the moment of conception, two separate people, this mother and her male child.

Lucia proceeded to make Maria more comfortable as Isabela moved to the door and motioned for Daniel to join them. He had been pacing outside while her father tried to convince him that all was well. It had not been an easy task. It was not Daniel's first time to become a father, but Penateka women did not allow their men within hearing distance until the birthing was done, so, even though he had been in this situation before, this was his first time to hear the agonizing cries of a woman he loved. His father-in-law tried to help, but Don Tomas could not help but remember the troubles Isabel had giving birth to Maria and their sickly, too early deceased son, and all of the miscarried attempts after. All Daniel could think of was the look on his friend's grieving face, admonishing him. "Tell her you love her, Daniel," Jake had said, "as soon as you can; as often as you can." So he could do nothing except pace as he listened to Maria's cries, and then, finally, to the cry of a babe. "Thank god," he prayed, when his mother-in-law appeared at the door with a smile on her face. He ran through the door to see that Maria, although pale and weak, was all smiles as she held the infant.

"Come say 'Hello,' to William Thomas," she said with a surprisingly strong voice, considering, letting him know he had a new son by using the name they had chosen together.

Daniel gently took the boy from her arms and watched his son look curiously around the room as though he could already focus his eyes. "This," said Daniel to himself once again, as he had twice before, when he had held a child of his own for the first time, "is as good as it gets."

"Your uncle and my husband," Isobel said approvingly, "but a long name for such a tiny one."

"W. T," Maria said softly, "will be long enough, at least for a while. She held her arm out and Daniel placed the boy back into them and kissed her forehead.

"Tu eres mi amor, mi querida," he whispered, *"para siempre* - for always."

Stone had enjoyed his lunch with Betsy Blake. She was not only pretty and petite, she had a simple way of looking at the world that was compassionate and nurturing. Interesting kid. Not quite in the same way that Khani Walters had been interesting, though. He had asked Betsy if she knew Khani.

"Khani Walters? Oh, yes, everybody knows Khani. Bobby grew up here. His family has been around a long time. It's a shame they split. I feel for those boys, but she just has more going on than he ever did. Bless Bobby. Even though he spent four years at the university, he seems like he's still stuck in high school."

"I think I know a few of the type. What university?"

"I forget. You're new to Texas. *The* university - UT - in Austin."

"They both went there?"

"That's right, both of them studying journalism; both of them getting jobs in Houston after they graduated. Bobby is still in Houston, but mostly doing free-lance these days. He's a pretty good guy, you know? Their lives just went in different directions. It happens."

Stone recalled that he had - once again - felt a sense of relief over hearing that Khani Walters was unattached, only now, as he was driving back to Sandy Creek, another wave of guilt started washing over him, crushing the pleasant feeling that he had been enjoying for a few hours, the first hours in a long time. Suddenly he was seeing Erin, and those kids he had so foolishly let go free.

He was moving deeper into this dark place when he had to hit his brakes, literally. Traffic was stopped just ahead. He pulled up at the back of a string of cars that inched along the two-lane highway, and the guilt was turning into frustrated anger. If he hadn't been near the top of a hill, on a two-lane highway, he might have turned on his siren and charged ahead. He was still in Gillespie County, barely, so was out of his jurisdiction, but as soon as they crossed the La Roca County line...

Then the road veered sharply to the right, still near the top of a high hill. A valley opened up below and to his left and suddenly the most predominant feature of the landscape in front of him was that gigantic pink granite outcropping. He could see the whole of it, clearly, sprawling across the valley in all its glory. That morning, when he had been driving down towards Fredericksburg from Sandy Creek, he had only caught shimmering glimpses, rising and disappearing as the road climbed and fell, but here, heading back north, it came upon you whole and sudden. It literally took his breath away. Stone realized that the reason for the traffic slow-down was that the cars were lined up to enter the park. The fact that the entrance was on the left side of the road, meant those who were entering were making left turns, and the oncoming traffic, headed south, made the process move even more slowly. He looked toward the rock. At first still feeling frustrated and angry over the delay and thinking the hell with the damned thing. As soon as the traffic cleared he was heading home; this place could wait for another day, when suddenly, all he could see was that rock, with the sun glistening off it in heat waves, and he heard Betsy's voice, back at the restaurant, saying, "It's just that being there makes you feel good," and he knew what she meant. He just felt peaceful.

71

The slowness of the line stopped bothering him. He settled in for the wait, and in the meantime, just took in as much as he could of that rock.

It actually appeared, from his angle, to be three rocks, all smooth rounded granite that shaded from pink into grey, and back to pink again. The first two domes had ribbons of green bushes running across them. The third, and largest, was almost completely bare, and except for a few spots, was completely smooth.

"One of the oldest spots in the country," Betsy had said, "billions of years old."

All three of those ancient domes protruded up through the relatively newer surface of sandy loam and limestone and stood in stark contrast to the surrounding landscape. As he inched closer he could see that there were occasional cracks in the surface, and smaller rocks and boulders that appeared to be the same weathered granite, some of them so rectangular they seemed almost man-made. His own state of mind grew more and more relaxed as he moved into the flow and the pace of the slowly progressing train of cars. There was, he noticed, a quality of pristine clarity, as though even his vision grew sharper. He felt completely caught up in each moment, almost as though time itself had ceased to exist. It seemed like no time later that he turned into the entrance of the park and the traffic flowed toward a small stone building and parking area.

"Deputy? How can I help you?"

Stone was jolted out of his reverie by a member of the park's security forces who had approached the van. "Stone," he replied, "La Roca County, but I'm not here officially, just wanted to see the place." He held out a five-dollar bill, the price for admission he had noted on a sign as he drove in.

"Thought you must be Sheriff White's new man. Don't worry about the fee. Just park in that lot to your right. You might want to stop inside the visitor's building and pick up a map. Enjoy your visit to Enchanted Rock State Park."

Stone gave a wry smile as he parked the van. Small towns. He already had a reputation here, too.

According to the map and brochure, there were several hiking trails. All of them seemed to begin at a small covered pavilion which held several display cases and a telescope. He stopped back at the van to pick up a canteen of fresh water, and headed for the pavilion.

As he entered the pavilion, he saw a large poster depicting the main domes. He stepped closer to read the caption: "My heart feels lighter," it began. "...my mind feels calmer and my senses feel tuned whenever I see that giant pink rock on the horizon..." He looked from the poster back to the rock itself. He knew what that writer had meant. He had been feeling it from the time he had rounded the hill and it came into his view. He then started down a path of stone steps toward the beginning of what the map called the Summit Trail, which would take him to the top of the tallest dome.

The climb had him a bit winded, but less so than he had expected when he had stood at the bottom of the dome. And from the moment he reached the summit, he knew it had been worth it, for he saw, below and around, the greatest expanse of open land he had ever seen. The valley, from this height, was much greener than it had seemed from below, the trees appearing to be much denser than they seemed when he had been down among them. The top of the dome was relatively flat, and he could walk around on it easily. There were a few indentations, some of them forming small pools with green vegetation. Looking south, he could see where Sandy Creek ran alongside the rocks, almost 500 feet below, and meandered northwest toward the little town he now called home. A soft breeze was blowing, and he could almost hear a whispering sound as it ruffled his hair.

Chapter 9

"Windsong."

Stone was startled by the voice. There were others climbing the trail, some alone, others in small groups of two or three, but he had hardly noticed them, he was so intent on his own experience. He looked around and saw a man standing next to him, looking out in the same direction. The man was old and grizzled, but at the same time, appeared to be quite strong and still muscular. He seemed friendly, and harmless enough, and Stone sensed something like that same peacefulness, much like the feeling that seemed to be coming from the breeze and the rock itself, emanating from the old man. "Windsong," he echoed the older man's word. "That whistle in the breeze, you mean?"

"More than a whistle. The Tonkawa and Comanche call it The Singing Rock, but Windsong isn't just a sound; he's a spirit."

"A spirit?"

"The keeper of the rock, an old indigenous entity, centuries old. He protects the rock from those who might want to do it harm."

"Who would want to harm a rock?"

"This isn't just any rock, although all rocks, everything, for that matter, that we think of as inanimate, have souls, just like animals and people." The old man, although rough in dress and appearance, spoke in a voice that implied an education, a worldly sort of knowledge, even while the notions he expressed seemed primitive. He was dressed in faded jeans, a flannel shirt, and a buckskin jacket that seemed older and more worn than the man himself. His beard was completely white; his long hair, pulled into a thin band at the nape of his neck, still had a few streaks of grey running through it. Stone remembered something Khani had said to him, that first day he met her, something about a hermit who lived somewhere in the valley. "If you want to learn more about reading sign and tracks," she had said, "he would be the one to teach you."

"Old Dan."

They looked at each other squarely, then. Stone was drawn to the man's eyes, light, blue-grey eyes that were starting to crinkle in amusement. "Joshua Stone," he grinned back. "It seems we both have reputations."

Stone was startled at that one. Could this old hermit read his thoughts? He liked the guy already, but wasn't quite sure whether to trust him or not. "I heard your name from Khani Walters. Where did you hear mine?"

"An old man hears a lot of things, sometimes just by listening."

It was an evasive answer, but the more Stone looked into Old Dan's eyes, the more he felt at ease with him. "Listening is good," he found himself saying, "In my job, it's a necessity. I would like to know more about this place, and I'm willing to listen, if you're willing to speak."

"This place?"

"Hell, the whole damn Hill Country," Stone laughed. "But I'm willing to start with where we're standing."

"Okay, for starters, she's called "Big Rock.""

"She?"

"Oh, yes, she is decidedly a female rock. Her little brothers will attest to that." He turned toward the west, gesturing with his chin, "The one you see there is called Little Rock, and the one to the east," he turned, and gave a similar gesture, "the smallest one, is called Freshman Mountain."

"The smallest one is a mountain."

Old Dan gave out a chortle. "Different people have different perspectives. We each have our own way of naming things. And the truth is that they are all one. Like islands that seem separate on the surface, but under the sea, are all connected, only here, the projections are on land. Just like all of our limited human perspectives, what we see is only a small part of a single, interconnected whole. This entire area rests on a giant batholith that runs underground for a hundred square miles." His tone shifted toward a lighter direction; the crinkles around his eyes deepened as he chuckled, "I've heard it said that this is the largest natural dome in the country...that doesn't have Confederate generals carved on it."

Stone was puzzled for a minute, then remembered and laughed, "Stone Mountain in Georgia. My old man took us there on vacation when I was a kid. Claimed it was named after our ancestors."

Dan chuckled back. "Stone is an interesting surname. It fits well with this countryside. You should feel at home here." He grew more serious again as he said, "but the main thing, for today, anyway, might be to remember that whatever the names or size, the highest and most powerful point of this rock has a feminine spirit. In this world, that is a power we foolishly neglect. We are standing on our mother, who gave birth to all of us, one painful step at a time."

75

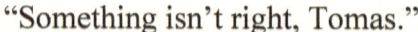

"Something isn't right, Tomas."

"What makes you think so?"

"It's taking too long. It didn't take this long before."

"Every birth is different, Daniel," Tomas tried to reassure his son-in-law, but the truth was, he was worried as well. Maria's confinement had begun before dawn, and it was now mid-afternoon.

"Not this kind of different. I can hear it in her cries." It was more than that, he knew. He could almost feel Maria's pain. He could sense her fear, and her fatigue.

And then, it came again, this one more intense and prolonged than ever.

He couldn't take his feelings of helplessness any longer; he started toward the house.

"Daniel, no..." Tomas tried to hold him back, but it was no use.

He ran toward the house, taking the steps several at a time, and pushed open the door into the birthing room. What he saw sent his head reeling.

The sheets and Maria's gown were red with her blood, her face as white as the pillows behind her back. Over Isabela's and Lucia's protestations, he went to her and knelt at her side. Her eyes were glazing, her breathing shallow.

"Maria!" he called to her.

Her eyes quickened a little, then. She knew he was near. "Daniel?" Her voice was so week it frightened him even more.

"Daniel," Isabela told him, "you must leave." He could hear the fear and fatigue in her voice as well.

"No." This came from Lucia. "You are here now," she said to Daniel, "so stay and be of help." Lucia's voice was grave, but controlled. She knew what she was doing.

"How?" he asked.

"Stay with Maria. Keep talking to her. Isabela, you come and help me."

Isabela looked uncertain, but she handed Daniel the damp cloth she had been using to wipe her daughter's face and moved toward to the foot of the bed.

Daniel took his wife's hand and wiped her forehead.

Her eyes were half-closed. She seemed to hear him calling her name, but was having difficulty focusing, and then, her face began tensing again and her hand gripped his, more and more tightly as her back arched, and her moan became a cry of intense agony.

The feeling of powerlessness grew until it was almost overwhelming.

"Keep talking to her," Lucia said sharply.

"I am here *querida*. Just hold onto my hand," he told her, and added, fearing that it was a lie, "All will soon be well."

Eventually, the spasm lessened, and Maria's grip on Daniel's hand slackened, but it was clear she could not take much more. He spoke to her again, looking into her face for a sign that she could hear him.

Lucia was clearly worried, but still calm. "The baby is turned the wrong way, and the water bag has come loose and is blocking the way. Isabela, when the next pain begins, you will need to help her."

Isabela nodded. She seemed to know what it was that she must do. She moved toward her daughter's stomach and laced her hands on either side.

Maria stiffened again, and the wracking cry tore at Daniel, but he held her hand and continued to speak to her, taking strength from Lucia's calm directions.

Finally he heard the midwife's relief as she called out, "I've got it."

The pain had lessened once again, but it restarted almost immediately.

"One more, Maria," Lucia reassured her. "It is almost done."

It was as though the four of them were one entity, working together to get this thing over. Maria choked out one more cry, and then collapsed.

Daniel could barely hear the wail of the infant. All he could focus on was the slight rise and fall of Maria's chest. She was breathing. That was all that mattered.

"*Es una bebita*," Isabel's voice was full of tears. "You have a daughter, my child."

Maria's lips moved, then, and Daniel leaned down to hear her. "Magdalena," she whispered, trying to smile. Her eyes closed and her breath grew more even. She seemed to be sleeping peacefully.

He did not know how much later it was before he heard Lucia say, "The bleeding has stopped."

He looked up, then, and saw that Isabela had wrapped the baby in a blanket, and was smiling at her. The tiny bundle was actively moving, and crying in protest at the swaddling.

"Lucia?"

"Let your wife rest now, Daniel. You daughter is healthy, and Maria will likely be well herself, in time."

Isabela came around and placed the bundle in his arms. "Magdalena?"

Daniel managed a smile for his mother-in-law. "Magdalena Isabela." He looked down and saw his daughter's blue eyes, looking around curiously at her new world, a tiny fist finding its way toward her pink mouth. "Little Maggie."

"Enough now." Lucia was firm as she looked toward the intruder in this place of women. "Let us take care of them. You go and tell Don Tomas he has a granddaughter."

Stone pushed his booted feet into the stirrups, partly to stretch, but mostly to rest his thighs and backside. He had to admit, though, he was slowly getting used to riding. Sitting astride a horse gave him a better view of the countryside, if nothing else. It had been a couple of weeks now, since he had run into Dan at Enchanted Rock. Since then, the two of them had been intent on solving the mystery of the disappearing cattle from Khani Walters' ranch. In the process, Stone was not only learning to ride, he was learning more about these hills, the terrain, and how to read what he saw. He could now tell the difference between live oak, cedar, and mesquite trees, and the difference between a dry wash and a draw. He could not only tell the difference between a cactus and a Yucca plant, he could distinguish the different kinds of cacti, from a prickly pear to a claret, and all the odd local varieties in between. Unlike Dan, he could not see how old a track was, or what type of shoe a horse had been wearing, although he could tell if it had been shod or not. He had mostly learned to get a feel for just how green he was, and how lucky he was to have run into Dan - if luck was what it was. He couldn't help but remember Khani's comment the day he first met her. "He's a hermit that lives somewhere back in the hills," she had said. "No one knows just where..." It seemed an odd coincidence that the man in question had turned up a few weeks later.

They had been riding toward the top of a high ridge, just south of Granite Hill, an outcropping of granite boulders all appearing to have been piled on top of one another, many of them rounded or cylindrical. Stone pointed out one in particular that seemed to have been carved into the shape of a small boat.

"Nature is an artist," Dan replied. "She uses the rain and wind like we use chisels and brushes." He leaned forward over the horn of his saddle, admiring the natural beauty in the formations all around them. He was quiet for a bit before he said, "Maybe it's like Michelangelo is supposed to have said."

"About David?"

"That's the one. What was it? He just chipped away everything that wasn't David? Maybe that's what happens with nature, the soul of the stone is inherent, and the water just washes away what didn't belong to the rock in the first place."

Dan suddenly grew quiet. He tilted his head as though he was listening to something that Stone couldn't hear. Then he said, "Rider coming."

"Problem?"

Dan shook his head. "J. T."

Stone continued to look around, not seeing or hearing anything.

Then, Dan let out a low whistle, sounding almost like a bird, and motioned for Stone to be quiet and listen. Then he heard, very faintly, an echo of the same sound, but it was several minutes more before the horseman appeared from the other side of the ridge.

"J. T?"

Dan nodded, "Khani's father."

As the man pulled closer, he turned toward Stone. "You'd be Mack's new deputy."

"Joshua Stone." He held his hand out to the gentleman, and noted that "gentleman" was indeed the proper term.

The man sat straight in his saddle, and looked Stone straight in the eye. There was something in his demeanor that quietly bespoke integrity. "My daughter speaks well of you," the man said as he took Stone's outstretched hand in a firm grip, "and Mack White is an old friend, so, welcome to Sandy Creek." He turned toward Dan, then. "Your hearing is as sharp as ever, old friend. It's good to see you."

The phone in Stone's pocket began to vibrate. At first he thought it might be about his twins, but was relieved to see another familiar name in the caller ID box. "Jeannie. What's up?"

"Hey, Josh," came Rayjean's drawling voice over the phone, "Mack just got a call from Betsy Blake down in Fredericksburg and said I should let you know about it."

"Shoot, kid."

They've been getting reports there in Gillespie County, too, about cattle disappearing. Seems like the same M-O as the one here, broken or cut fences, a few steers missing, not many tracks to follow. Looks like we got us a rustling ring going on."

"Any more details?"

"She's faxing a copy of the report over right now. I can email it to you as soon as it's in."

"That'll be great, Jeannie. Thanks."

"It's more what the report doesn't say than what little it does." That came from J. T. The three men had finished checking out the area around Granite Hill and had ridden to a line cabin so that they could talk and eat something for lunch. Stone was glad to have his feet on the ground again, and was more than impressed by what J. T. had called a "cabin." It was actually a small stone house, furnished with a couple of bunks, comfortable sitting area, and a complete, if compact kitchen - stocked with canned foods and, best of all, a refrigerator with cans of cold Shiner beer. J. T. had pulled some buns and sausage from the freezer, popped them into the microwave with a bit of barbeque sauce, and they were sitting around the table, eating, and talking about the news from Fredericksburg.

"Like what?"

"Like signs of where the steers were taken, what was done with them when they got them to wherever."

Dan added, "Stone and I have ridden every square mile in that corner, starting from the cut fence and circling out. What tracks there were led into the rocks, and then nothing. And there wasn't one sign of a fire, much less evidence of anything like a running iron."

"I can vouch for the mileage," Stone said, shifting a little on the hard chair.

J. T.'s eyes flashed that glint of humor again. "Getting saddle-worn pretty quickly, son?"

"Let's just say Dan believes in teaching through experience."

J. T. gave him a sympathetic smile. "Back to the fires, or lack of them, and add that there are no signs that the cattle were driven away." He smiled a little again, in Stone's direction, and said, "Check that. I should have said 'herded.'"

"Like on horseback?"

"Right."

"Meaning they were trucked out." Stone took a bite of his sandwich and chewed as he thought before adding, "except there were no truck ruts, either."

"Which would explain why they had been herded into the rocks," Dan pointed out.

"Where the tracks disappear," Stone was beginning to get a clearer picture.

"A few head at a time," J. T. finished.

"Smaller trucks?" Stone asked. He took a swig from the beer bottle before answering his own question, "off-road type with a high ground clearance."

"Unimogs," J. T. offered. "We used them in the Army to reach remote installations."

Dan looked at him quizzically. "Unimog?"

"UNIversal-MOtor-Gerät. Gerät is just a German word that means a device. Unimogs are made by Mercedes-Benz. They can be adapted to almost any terrain, and for purposes ranging from military to agriculture. Modern technology for adapting a centuries old crime."

"So, we've got them off the range and onto the highway," Dan added. "Where then?"

Stone answered, thinking out loud, "a central location. A meat processing plant?"

"It would get rid of the brands."

"But easy to track." J. T. reached into the large bag of potato chips sitting in the center of the table as he shook his head. "They wouldn't need to bother with altering the brands if they had paperwork to indicate ownership."

"Easily forged." This came from Stone. "More modern technology. So, we've got the beef, we've got the papers, what next?"

"Mexico?" Dan asked.

"Most likely," J. T. answered.

"But where do they cross the border?"

"From here? Probably through San Antonio, south to Corpus, then down the coast to Brownsville, over the river into Matamoros."

"And from there, they could find plenty of places where no questions would be asked."

They all seemed to be in accord. It was Old Dan who brought the group back to reality. "Well, now, we've been doing a nice lot of speculation. It seems a good theory, but how do we prove it?"

Stone spoke up then. He felt more at ease than he had since he had left New York. "That would be my job."

"Okay, Deputy Stone. Just what is your next move?"

"More technology. More and better."

"How, Josh, and what?"

"Easy enough," Stone smiled. "We just catch them red-handed." He was a happy man at that point. This was a job he knew how to do blindfolded.

"You seem to know what you have in mind." J. T. looked at Stone with a growing respect. He excused himself from the table, then, saying something about the effects of a couple of beers. Stone looked after him, thinking similar thoughts. "The man knows his stuff," he commented to Dan.

"Military background," Dan told him. "Career officer when he was younger."

"Yeah?"

Dan nodded. "He loved it. The discipline; sense of order. It was his life. And he was very good at it. Made it to full colonel. Then he came back from his last tour of Vietnam with a little dark-eyed toddler."

"Khani."

"Since then, she has been his life."

Jake woke quickly from a deep sleep, trying, in the first few moments, to figure out what was different. Then he felt it, the slender, feminine arm that lay across his chest. For an instant, he thought it was

Karin. Then he remembered. He eased the woman's arm back and tried to slip from the bed without waking her, slipped on his pants and padded barefoot into the kitchen, put a stick of wood into the potbelly of the stove and started making a pot of coffee.

"You always wake up so early?"

"Always have." He felt a little awkward, carrying on a conversation with her. The Fredericksburg widow was the town's schoolteacher. She and her young son had moved to the new community shortly after it was established. Her relationship with Jake had been going on for a while, but this was the first night she had spent in his home. For that matter, it was the first time they had slept together for a whole night. He was feeling more than a little guilt, even though it had been almost two years since Karin's death. He turned toward Molly, trying to think of something appropriate to say, in what still felt like an inappropriate situation. "Coffee will be ready soon," he finally said.

She made it easy for him. She smiled at him as she fastened the buttons of her dress. "No, Jake. Thank you, but it will be turning daylight soon, and I should get home before it does."

Now he felt guilty for slighting her. "The boys are both over at the Wilkes's, if they all haven't already left for the lake. I know that Chase has been excited about this fishing trip from the time Pastor Wilkes came up with the idea."

"Adam, too. It's nice that Isaiah Wilkes looks after the children here the way he does. He is a good man, as well as being a good preacher. Sandy Creek is lucky to have him." She smiled and shook her head. "It's the rest of the town I was thinking about."

Now he felt even more guilty. He walked over to her, lifted her chin toward his and gave her a gentle kiss. "You're a good woman, Molly Sloane. You deserve better than this."

"And you, Sheriff Holder, are a good man. Too good sometimes. We both agreed that this was what we wanted, and we both know it is all either of us is ready for." She smiled, then, and returned his kiss. "Last night was very nice, though."

"A hell of a lot more than nice."

She laughed, then, her eyes twinkling. "You're right, Jake. 'Nice' had nothing to do with it." She turned to leave through the kitchen door, then looked back and added softly, "See you again soon."

"Yeah," Jake nodded back, his mood lifting, "soon is good."

The knock on the front door of the small town house came almost immediately after. "Who in hell?"

The knock came again, and a voice, "Jake?"

"Daniel?" He opened the door quickly to let his friend in. "Is everything okay," his voice grew more worried, "Maria?"

"Maria will be fine, Jake. She is getting stronger every day. That's not why I'm here."

"You're out early, friend."

"Uh-huh." Daniel's eyes gave away the serious tone in his voice. "And so is the widow Sloane."

"You might keep quiet about that."

"No problem," Daniel assured his friend as he came into the house.

"Including Maria?"

"Hell, Jake. Maria told me last week."

"Shit."

"Relax. People in this town are more open than you might think. A lot of us are saying, 'It's about time' - for both of you."

"But not for Chase or Little Adam."

"People here will respect that, I would think. Where are they, anyway?"

They were in the kitchen by this time. Jake handed Daniel a cup of coffee. "Pastor Wilkes and a couple of deacons at the church took the boys fishing. They all stayed at the Wilkes's last night."

"That's a good thing." Daniel smiled, "It won't be long before W. T. will be old enough for me to teach him. Now that he's found his feet, he runs faster than he can walk."

"...and if he slows down, he trips himself. Chase was like that. I remember how Karin..." He brought himself up short. Remembering still hurt, especially when it sneaked up on him. "So what does bring you out this early?"

"This does." Daniel held up a slim iron rod with a hook at one end.

It came to Jake that his friend had been holding it all along. He knew immediately what it was. "Running iron." He took the iron in his hand and studied it. "Where did you find it?"

"In the rocks, northwest side of Granite Hill, near the stone circle."

"Anything else?"

"Remains of a fire; tracks leading around and south."

"How many head are missing?"

84

"At least ten, probably more. Diego is still checking."

Jake was still contemplating the iron rod in his hand. Some ranchers preferred to use them for branding their own cattle, although a fixed brand was more common, especially now that the brands were being registered. These days, a running iron was mostly used by rustlers. "You know, though, Daniel," Jake's voice had picked up a twist of his Kentucky roots, which was a sure sign that he was getting ready to speak with his tongue lodged in his cheek, "I seem to recall a couple of young wranglers who managed to build up a bit of a herd of their own..."

Daniel wasn't in the mood at that moment. "We never used a running iron, Jake, and the Double R was never seared into a calf that had another man's brand on it.

"That's true, and they were all on open range, but mostly because Sam Maverick didn't bother to brand his own stock."

"And didn't really care if he lost a few head. Mostly because he didn't deem them to be of much monetary value."

"Driving them into Louisiana seemed liked a lot of work for not much profit." Jake agreed.

"It was a common - and perfectly legal - practice. This," he took the iron back from Jake and held it up in front of him, "is a long way from legal."

"You said the tracks headed south?"

"Headed toward the Nueces, and probably further beyond."

"Shit." Jake used that word again; then he added, *"Cheno."*

"Cheno?"

"Juan Nepomuceno Cortina y Goseacochea; *'Cheno'* Cortina to his friends."

"Your friend?"

"We got drunk together more than once, while I was still with the Rangers."

"You stopping there?"

"The Cortinas and Goseacocheas are old aristocratic families, south of the Nueces. Together they control most of the land along the Rio Grande around Brownsville and Matamoros, or, at least, they did, before Guadalupe-Hidalgo."

"The treaty that ended the war with Mexico."

"Once Texas became a state, a lot of old issues with Mexico had to be resolved."

"And the *tejanos* got caught in the middle."

"And Cheno among them. Mixed loyalties. He fought with Mexico during the war, but today he's considered the head of the Democratic party in South Texas. Only now there's a group of local politicians and judges in Brownsville who are working to rob the *tejanos* of their rights."

"I've heard about that part."

"Cheno has become their hero and leader - kind of like Robin Hood in old England. He and his followers steal cattle from the Anglos and give the meat to the struggling *tejanos*."

"Only the Double R is just nominally Anglo, and Don Tomas is one of them."

"Technically, but the Pinedas are more Spanish than Mexican. They've been loyal to Texas from the beginning."

"But we're on their side in this, Jake – both of us. You're still a partner in the Double R, even if you haven't had the time to be active."

Jake stroked his chin for a minute before responding. "It's pretty quiet in Sandy Creek right now, until this. Give me a few days off. I could do with them about now."

"I'll bet you could."

Jake ignored the comment and went on, "If I head south and can find him, I think I can convince Cheno that we aren't part of his problem. I doubt that he is in favor of his followers coming this far north anyway. Give me a little time to see if I can handle things without escalating them."

"Done. I don't like the way Austin is dealing with the *tejano* population these days. It sounds like the situation in Brownsville is more of the same crap. Need someone to look after Chase while you're gone?"

"I could ask Molly, but..."

"I hear you. Part of me says it might be better for you to face that, but consider it done. Maria and W.T. will be happy to have Chase around for a week or so."

Chapter 10

"What's in the paper bag?"

"Feel free to take a look. It is your kitchen, after all."

Stone reached into the bag and pulled out a bottle. "Zinfandel Don Tomas – Rancho de Pineda Viñedo Orgánico – Texas Hill Country," he read aloud, "A winery in Texas?"

"One of the best wineries in Texas."

"There's more than one?"

"Not quite so many as many as New York, but at least the quality."

"Right here in the hills?"

"Most of them are around here."

"And you say that this Rancho de Pineda is one of the best?"

"You tell me after you've had a glass."

"So, what's the occasion?"

"I'm cooking you a celebratory dinner, that's the occasion." Khani was clearly very pleased with herself, and with him. "You, Deputy Joshua Stone, late of the NYPD and newest hero of the State of Texas, at least in these parts, have just solved your first major crime bust since you left New York."

"Just a job."

"Just a job, Josh? The biggest cattle-rustling ring in the hill country for the millennium?"

"Which is just now approaching its third year, Khani. Big deal."

"Very big deal. Actually, there is another reason to celebrate, to go along with. And the two of them are related."

"Keep going."

"You are now looking at the newest news reporter for the Sandy Creek Gazette."

"Hey, you did it. Good for you. It will be fun, knowing at least one reporter that I like and respect."

"Let's hope it stays that way after tonight. Remember, I said there was a connection. While we do dinner and get tipsy, I plan to coax the whole story out of you."

"What whole story?"

"Oh, come on. I know that you managed to get infrared cameras working at their central camp, but how did you find it? What other technological cop secrets did you use?"

"Best we stay away from cop secrets. These guys haven't gone to trial yet." He continued to look through the contents of the paper bag. "Pasta? Roma tomatoes? Fresh basil? Something tells me we are not having fajitas." He pulled out a butcher wrapped object and read the label. "Extra-lean ground beef. A new chili recipe?"

"Basil-scented chili. Sure. I heard you tell my dad that you hadn't had a decent bowl of spaghetti and meat sauce since you left New Jersey. I'm here to prove to you that we can cook anything you might eat on the whole upper east coast, and do it as well or better."

"Great, when do we do lobster."

"We get seafood, dork. We aren't that far from Corpus and the Gulf. Just wait 'til you taste my blue crab."

"The crab is blue? And I'm 'Dork' now?" Stone teased her, "I thought this dinner was supposed to be in my honor."

"It is. That's why Leticia is feeding our children and taking them to the movies. This evening is about us, and our professional achievements."

Stone insisted, a few hours later, on doing the dishes alone. "You cooked; I clean. Did I tell you that you were right?"

"About what?"

"You, Khani Walters, cook a mean beef sauce."

"We raise the beef. That might be considered cheating."

"However. Besides, you were right about the wine, and it was perfect for the sauce."

"Still cheating. We grow the grapes – and make the wine."

"Shit. You really are somebody around here, aren't you?"

Khani gave him a modest shrug.

Well, whoever you are, the dinner was great. Thanks."

"You're welcome, again. You did tell me earlier."

He loaded the last dish into the dishwasher and started it. His work done, he turned to face Khani, and started to feel a little awkward. "Kids ought to be getting out of the movie soon."

Khani walked closer to him and smiled. "Didn't I tell you? Leticia is keeping all of them at the Sunday house for the night." She walked even closer, and put her hands on his shoulders, then reached her lips toward his.

He responded to her, gently at first, then with more fervor.

She asked him, though the kisses, "Is this what you want, Josh?"

"What I want? Shit, Khani, what in hell do you think you're feeling?"

She smiled, "Okay, I'll rephrase my question. Are you ready for this?"

He dropped his head to her neck, then took her shoulders and moved back, a little, so he could look at her face. "I guess that depends."

"Depends?"

"On just what 'this' is." he looked more closely at her face, stroked a strand of her hair behind her ear. "How about you? It hasn't been all that long since you and Bobby split."

"So if you're asking if I'm ready for another 'lifelong commitment,' the answer is 'No.' I doubt you want that either, at this point. You said a little while ago that you respected me. Would you still?" She grinned a little. "In the morning? After I've thrown myself at you?"

He moved his hand back to her hair and ran his fingers through it, reaching for the back of her head and pulling her closer.

"Respect isn't exactly what I have in mind at the moment."

A soon as she woke, the next morning, Khani realized she was alone. There was a faint smell of coffee coming from the kitchen. She raised herself to her elbows and looked around. She and Stone had obviously been in a hurry to undress. Their clothes lay all about the room, especially on the floor between the bed and the doorway. She found her underwear and the plaid flannel shirt that Stone had been wearing. She appropriated it, and started down the hall to the kitchen, led by the aroma of freshly brewed coffee. She poured herself a cup, wandered a bit, and finally tried the door that led into the back yard.

A long porch stretched across the length of the house. The yard itself reminded her of her own. Swings, a shortened basketball hoop, and a slide, and in Stone's case, in one corner, a playhouse for Chellie. It reminded her that they both had primary responsibilities to their children, no matter what might - or might not - be developing between the two of them.

Stone was standing on the corner of the porch, leaning against the post. He was barefoot and shirtless, wearing the same faded jeans he had on the night before. He turned in her direction as she walked toward him. His face, in the dawn light, was not easy to read.

"So," she started gingerly, "how do you feel?"

"In truth? A little bit guilty. Mostly because, as hard as I try, I can't manage to feel as guilty as I think I ought to feel about last night."

"About last night. Wasn't that a movie title?"

"I think so, maybe, but I'm not that sure, because all I can focus on is how much better you look in that shirt than I ever did." He took a sip of his coffee before he asked, "So, how about you. How do you feel?"

"In truth? I feel...laid." She grinned broadly as she said it.

Stone couldn't help but laugh. He asked her, "So, when do you expect Leticia will be bringing the kids back?"

Khani looked at the sky, which was still only beginning to brighten. "Oh, I would guess, a couple of hours, at least."

Stone set his cup on a small table, walked over to Khani, took her cup and set it down before he picked her up in his arms and carried her back to the bedroom.

Daniel threw a coin onto the counter at Belle's Place and took a sip from the glass that the bartender had placed in front of him. He took a look at his surroundings. Gold and red velvet. There was no mistaking the purpose for this "house," he thought to himself. It was early enough in the day that he was alone. He had decided the best thing was to not attempt to hide his entrance. Let people think what they might. He knew his reasons for being here.

He could hear Lucia's words still. "She will recover, Daniel, *this time*."

"This time?" He had made it a question, but he was sure he knew the answer.

"Once a birth like this one happens, it is likely it will happen again, only the problem will be worse, and more dangerous." He heard the rest of Lucia's warning ring in his ears. "Maria should not have another child. *It would probably kill both of them*."

"Well, I figured you would find your way through my door eventually, Mr. Redstone. I didn't expect it would be quite this soon."

"Word gets around fast, Belle." He turned to face the woman. In contrast to her "place," Belle Dawson had a look of gentility about her.

90

Her silver hair was pulled back in a simple knot; her dress was discreet, and obviously expensive.

"So, how is your wife?"

"Recovering. She is a strong woman, and determined to look after our home and children, no matter what. She will be well soon."

"But not well enough, I hear. It's earlier than we generally do business, but I can get one of the girls..."

"I'm here to see you, Belle."

"I'm flattered, I suppose, but I don't..."

"You misunderstand, Belle. I'm here on a different kind of business."

"And just what would that be, then, Mr..."

"Call me Daniel. Is there a place we can talk privately?"

She looked a little puzzled, and suspicious, but finally gestured to a door near the back. "My office, then...Daniel."

Unlike the garish furnishings in the main bar, Belle's office suited her appearance and demeanor. It reassured Daniel. He felt he was doing the right thing, and his first impressions of this businesswoman had him feeling more so.

"I'll get right to the point. The gossip mongers have clearly been working quickly. As you already seem to know, my wife must not have another child."

"People have voiced their suspicions. I take it you are looking for some - special arrangements?"

"I love my wife, Belle, and am extremely fortunate in that she loves me back. There could never be another woman who would...suit me."

"Then why are you here, Daniel?

He had a feeling she knew, but was not going to say it herself. "I don't know if you are aware, but I spent my childhood in New Orleans." He let that sink in, then continued. My family owned a merchant shipping line, and several ships. Let us just say that I - came of age? - as an apprentice seaman on one of those vessels."

"Perhaps I should get to the point, Daniel. If you are looking for a sheath, there are better and more economical places."

"A sheath protects from diseases, and, to a lesser degree, from conception. That answer is not the one I'm looking for."

"Then perhaps you could be more specific."

"Among the many sea merchants I came across were more than a few sponge fishermen. It was my understanding that the smaller sponges were sold - at a high price - for a particularly valuable purpose."

She came out with it then, whether it was because she was beginning to trust him, or was just tired of the game, Daniel was not sure.

"You want to procure a pessary for your wife."

"Precisely."

"The most effective ones are wrapped in silk. Pure silk is most expensive."

"Cost is not an object, Belle. Effectiveness is."

"So, you were thinking you could come in here, purchase this device, and go home?"

Daniel shrugged. "Something like that."

She shook her head. "One would think that...*enlightened*...men would have a better understanding of a woman's body. We come in different shapes and sizes, Daniel - including our most intimate parts."

"And this means?"

"Your wife will have to come to me herself."

"That could present a problem."

"I can only imagine. Does she have a midwife she can trust?"

"She does, but they are both Catholic. I will have to do some persuading."

"Then, Daniel, if you wish to do business, I suggest you get to it."

"It is out of the question."

"Maria, give me time to explain..."

"It is against the law of God, Daniel."

"God, Maria, or merely the church?"

"*Merely* Daniel? The church is the instrument of God. If we deny one, we deny the other."

"Which church, Love?" Daniel asked the question gently. "Jake is Lutheran, my mother's family is Anglican. The Penateka have no 'church,' but that doesn't keep them from following their concept of God, in their own way."

Maria was silent for a moment, before she spoke, "This is not necessary."

Maria, I miss you."

"You think I do not? Daniel, look at me. I am well now. I am strong. Lucia isn't certain there would be problems with the next child..."

"The odds are that there could be. I will not take that chance."

The look in Maria's eyes was hard for him to take. He knew how much she wanted to have their life back. And she clearly knew, too, that eventually, he would be compelled to find another answer to their dilemma. If he could only convince her that what he was suggesting was not wrong. He took a deep breath, and started again, "Maria, do you believe that Karin Holder's death was God's will? Do you believe that her death was a punishment?"

"Of course not. Karin was the soul of goodness. There was nothing she could have done to deserve dying, leaving Jake and Chase to go on without her."

"Jake, then. Was God punishing him, by taking away what he loved most in the world? Jake's job requires a gun, and he has to be willing to use it. He has used it, to protect the people he has a duty to protect."

"Jake is as good and fine a man as you are. No, and besides, Karin and her baby were completely innocent. God would not use them to punish Jake."

"God loved them, then."

"You know He did. He loves all of us."

"And you and I, Maria. We love each other, and we are husband and wife. Expressing that love is a natural and beautiful thing - a sacred thing. Would a loving God deny us that passion?"

He could see her confusion. "It is taking a life."

"No, love. It is preventing a conception that could well lead to a death - your death, and the death of an innocent child."

He could see she was considering his words. She wanted - needed - for them to be free to make love as much as he did. "You said we would need Lucia's help. How could we expect her to agree?"

"Lucia has seen this...senseless wrong...too many times. She is a practical woman. I do not believe she will take much convincing."

Molly Holder had the most delightful laugh. Maria could not help but laugh with her. It was such an exquisitely beautiful day that laughter almost had to be a part of it.

They were watching the three boys, Chase, Adam, and "Dub" as they wrestled together on the ground. W. T. was proving to be too much of a mouthful for little Maggie to pronounce, now that she was learning to speak. Dub was as much as she could manage, so Dub her brother had become.

Dub was big and strong for a five-year-old, and was holding his own with his eight-year-old companions. Maggie had toddled along behind them, keeping a safe distance. She couldn't quite decide whether to move closer and play with them, or focus on the raggedy doll she held tightly to her chest.

The bluebonnets were still blooming, here on this hill, in and among the rocks, the yucca plants, and the scraggily mesquite trees. There was a light breeze. It was still spring, for a while longer, before the summer heat, and the two families were enjoying a pleasant lull.

Even the grown men, who were mimicking the boys rough and tumble behavior with their game of words, seemed pleasant. Maria had long since realized that the long-running argument Daniel and Jake continued to hold when they had time to relax together was not a thing to worry about. The current topic was another matter, but it was just too good a day to worry about the future.

"He's going to lose this election, Jake."

"This is Sam Houston we're talking about, Daniel."

"He played around with those Know-nothings and the American Party when he supported Dickson in the last election. American party," Daniel shook his head. "White Americans, they mean. They call themselves 'native-born' but deny the rights of the real natives here, along with any immigrants who didn't come from England."

"He didn't have a whole lot of choices."

"Jake, your son is half German. I, your friend, am half Comanche, and my wife is one hundred percent Spanish. If the American Party takes hold here, what will that mean for all of us?"

"I agree, and if I thought Houston felt that way, he wouldn't have my support."

"Sam is being Sam. He will back whoever will promise him the most votes."

"We have to get elected if we are going to hold a public office, Daniel."

"I didn't see you having any trouble in the last election here in Sandy Creek. The town was pretty quick to show you their support without you having make promises you didn't plan on keeping."

"I ran for County Sheriff, Daniel. What other fool was willing to run against me."

"That's not the point."

"That's beside the point and you know it. How about you? I don't hear you going out and campaigning for Hardin Runnels."

"Hell, no. He'd have Calhoun's policies overrunning the state. Secession would be a given, and we would be at war for certain."

"So, Daniel, who do you support?"

"You know I'll be voting for Houston - for *governor*," he added emphatically, and then, even more emphatically, "*this* election. And I'll do what I can to get a bigger following for the Republican Party by the next presidential election."

"And you'll have as much success as you had with the Whig's. Democrats run this state, Daniel, whether we like it or not."

"One quarter of the population should not make policies for the other seventy-five percent of us."

"They have the means; they have the power."

Daniel shook his head again. "Extremists - on both ends - are running this country, and they're running it straight into the ground."

"No argument there. It looked, for a while after 1850 and the Compromise, that we were working toward a solution, but that ended last year."

"When Congress passed the Kansas-Nebraska Act, they threw the whole country into chaos. Democrats, Whigs, both split on the slavery issue, Calhoun and the Southern Democrats managing to take control of the one while the other faltered."

"And Sam's opposition to it has damaged his chances here in Texas. The Union is in real trouble."

"I find myself thinking more in terms of when the war comes, rather than if. There will be some hard decisions to be made, Jake, especially here in the hills."

"All I know is that I can't fight for any man's right to own another. The South is intent on pushing its citizens into taking that stand. I won't be able to stand with them, that's certain."

Daniel nodded. He and his friend might argue fine points, but neither of them questioned where the other stood on the issue of slavery. The South had harnessed itself to this evil, and was bent on forcing it on to the rest of the country. The real battle, they both knew, was between the old agricultural world and the new industrial one, and they both knew which would eventually win. They were both southerners, aware that the world of their childhood was no longer viable, and they differed only, when they differed, in their ideas about how to get through the chaos of there changing times. All Daniel knew was that he was bound to this valley, and to protecting its secrets. And he knew that, even though Jake knew nothing about those secrets, his friend would stand with him.

Both men felt the stir of the breeze going stronger. They looked around at their families and the wildflowers that were hanging tenaciously to these last days of spring, and knew that, in spite of the beauty that hung in the air around them, the peacefulness that pervaded their valley was too soon about to end.

Daniel was working in the corral and had seen the horse approaching from a distance. He recognized the rider as he grew closer. The man dismounted as he drew near the house, and Maggie ran outside to greet her "Uncle" Jake, who picked her up and held her close as she planted her five-year-old's kisses all over his face. He reluctantly set her on the ground and walked his horse toward that corral, and was loosening the saddle as Daniel walked over.

"Be prepared, Daniel," he warned his friend, "you are going to have to fight them all away in a few more years." He shook his head with a smile. "Between those green eyes and Maria's hair and skin, every man in the valley is going to be wrapped around her finger."

"Including her father and brother." He didn't want to change the subject, but he had to. "Molly and the boys know you're back?"

"Not yet. I figured I needed to stop here first."

"Give your horse a rest. Let's go inside."

Maria was waiting for them when they entered the sitting room. She looked at Jake's face and said, "The news is not good, is it?"

"The news is what we expected, Maria."

"Yes. I guess I was hoping for a miracle."

"How did Sam take it?"

"Hard. They are probably going to insist that he sign a loyalty oath, and he will refuse, and Edward Clark will take over as governor until the next election."

Maria shook her head sadly, "When General Houston won the last election, it looked like a more moderate government might be able to keep this from happening."

"That was before Harper's Ferry."

"And on top of that, here in the state, that long drought last summer, and the fires over in Dallas County."

"Is there any chance that they really were set by rebellious slaves?"

"There is no way, at this point, to know for certain, Maria," Jake answered her, "but I was in Abe's store when a fire started, around the same time, in the same weather conditions, right here at home. We both saw it. A crate of matches just blew up in flames. If we hadn't been right on top of it, the whole store could have gone up with it."

"And maybe the whole town, Daniel added. "We had gone so long without rain, the creek was almost dry."

"And you're certain it was from the matches?"

"The match heads are made of phosphorus, Maria. If they get too hot, they can ignite, even if you don't strike them, and the fires in Dallas County were all in buildings where crates of matches would have been stored."

"And the war-mongers in East Texas were so intent on bringing secession about, it wouldn't be beyond them to make up the whole thing."

"Whatever the cause, those flames stoked the fires, literally. Hell, Daniel, there were eight of us. Eight sane men in a room of nearly two hundred, *eight* who were willing to speak out and vote for keeping the Union intact."

"So," Maria asked them, "what do we do now?"

"We go about our lives, love." Daniel pulled his wife toward him and lightly kissed her temple. "We just keep going and do the best that we can from day to day."

Jake nodded, "We do our jobs, and take it as it comes. Hell, it's all any of us can ever do. It's even more important now."

Chapter 11

Chase finished sweeping the jail floor and walked back into the office, closing the door behind him.

His father sat at the desk. "How are they holding up?"

"Okay, I guess. They're scared, I think."

"That's only natural, son."

"And hungry, I imagine."

Jake smiled at that. "And what makes you imagine that? Maybe you're a little hungry yourself?"

"Guess so," he laughed. Chase was tall for a thirteen-year-old, and was generally hungry, but it was getting close to lunch time. His stepmother would be coming by soon, with food for all of them, including the two prisoners who were sitting quietly in their cells. "Pa? Do we have to keep them here? They didn't really do anything wrong."

"Technically, Chase, what they did was wrong. According to Confederate law, at sixteen, all males living in the state are supposed to register and swear an oath of allegiance. They didn't."

"Fort Mason is a long ride from here. And their pa is away fighting with the frontier patrol. Somebody has to work the farm."

"I agree, son. That's why I've written a letter to Colonel McCullough, asking for a dispensation. In the meantime, they're safer here in the jail where the partisans can't get to them."

"Do you think the colonel will help?"

"I don't know son, the McCullough brothers were both friends of mine, when we all rode with the Rangers, but this war has caused a lot of old friendships to be broken. We will just have to wait and see."

About that time, the door opened, and Molly Holder came through with a large tray, covered with a checkered cloth. Chase and his dad both jumped up to help.

"Boy, am I glad to see you, Ma. I was getting pretty hungry."

Molly laughed, "You are always hungry, Chase. You and Adam both."

"Did Adam go out to the Double R?"

"Right after he finished his chores at the house. He will be helping Daniel and Diego with the last of the round-up, so he will probably stay there tonight."

"That's good. I wouldn't want him on the road late with the

partisans out and about."

"Adam and I can both look after ourselves, Pa."

"Don't say another word, Chase." Jake's voice was harsher than he had meant it to be, but he continued, "Don't even think it. If Captain Duff or any of his men were to run into you, they wouldn't be likely to ask your age. If either of you were to show any sign of resisting..." He didn't need to finish the sentence.

"Those boys over in Kerr County were innocent, Chase," Molly finished for Jake, "when two of them managed to escape, the other four were hung on the spot; no hearing, no trial. Their bodies were just dumped in the creek, and nothing done about it. Governor Lubbock has declared martial law here in the hills. He knows that we're mostly Union sympathizers, and that essentially makes us traitors in the eyes of the Confederacy."

Jake shushed her, and cocked his head sharply, listening to something.

Then Molly and Chase heard it, too. Horses, quite a few of them, were riding hard and coming closer.

"Stay inside," Jake said to the two of them, checked the pistol in his holster, and picked up another before going outside. Chase and Molly looked at each other without saying a word. They had no trouble hearing what was going on outside in the street.

"That's far enough," they heard Jake say.

The horses slowed to a stop. "You're holding two of our prisoners, Sheriff."

Partisan Rangers, Chase thought to himself.

"My prisoners," Jake said firmly, "And they stay here, at least until I've heard from Colonel McCullough."

"Captain Duff says we've waited long enough. We're here to take them to Fort Mason. They will be tried and hung for the traitors that they are.

"You best walk easy, Holder," another of them said. "We know where you stand."

"I'm an elected official, and I turned thirty-five before your first shave, so don't even start to go there, son."

"Ain't your son, but we know you got one, and besides, the age limit for conscription changed to forty-five last week. Guess you ain't had time to get the word. All you got to hide behind now is that badge, and we just might be able to do something about that. We know how you voted at the convention."

"I'm hiding behind a badge for my exemption. Every man in the state who owns at least fifteen slaves is hiding behind those numbers, and any man who can afford to buy a substitute is hiding behind his money. I'm sure you know the saying, 'It's a rich man's war, but it's the poor who fight it for them.' Just like those two boys in there. Their father is on the frontier, fighting to keep the Comanche from raiding your homes and property"

"That's not our problem, Sheriff."

"Of course not. Any more than it is for the bankers who will take over their farms when they can't make their payments, so don't try and talk to me about what's right and what's wrong. Just ride out and tell Captain Duff there will be no lynchings in Sandy Creek, or of any of our citizens as long as I'm in charge here."

"Guess we best see to it you ain't in charge no more, then." One of the partisans drew a pistol, but Jake was too quick for him. Other shots were fired. Chase could see through the window as his father spun around, regained his balance and fired back. By the time it was done, he had emptied both of his own pistols. A dozen of the partisans fell with him.

"That's good work, Adam." Daniel gave the boy a man's slap on his shoulder. "We will be able to get these head to Juan Cortinas, now, and he will get them past the Confederates."

About that time they both looked up to see two riders headed toward the ranch, riding fast. Too fast. It did not take Daniel long to recognize Molly and Chase.

"What the hell?"

Chase was on the ground first, running to Daniel as Adam helped his mother from her horse.

"They killed him, Uncle. The partisan bastards killed my father."

It took Molly a long time to cry. She sat in silence as Chase coolly recounted what had happened back in Sandy Creek. "After they shot Pa, the ones who were left really went wild. They got his keys and went into the jailhouse and pulled the boys out, and started to hang them, right there. Might of hung me, too, if Ma hadn't held me back. When Pastor Wilkes tried to stop him, one of them pulled out a bullwhip and started lashing him with it, and then, they hung him, too. After, they just left them there and rode out, hollering and shooting. On the way out, they set fire to the church." Chase's eyes stayed cold, hard, and dry through the whole recounting.

Nine-year-old Dub uncharacteristically held a tight arm around his little sister, Maggie, who, even at seven, was able to understand all too clearly what had happened to her Uncle Jake and the others.

That was one of the worst of the evils of war, Maria was later to tell Daniel. It took away the childhoods of the innocent young ones.

It was Daniel who turned out to be the first to show tears. Maria found him, at the end of the day, after the grieving family had been settled in, out by the corral, looking toward the rock as the sun set behind it.

"I did this to him. I called him my friend. Hell, he saved my life, and now I am responsible for his death."

"God in Heaven, how could you think so?"

"He left the rangers after Bandera Pass. He wanted no more part in the violence. He saw what that kind of close fighting did to a man. He saw his own sergeant slash my father's dead body into pieces..."

"I know the rest of this story. He saw you fall, as you fought with your father's people, and kept you hidden from the other Rangers until the battle was done, and gave you water, and tended your wound, so that you were able to recover and return to the Penateka. And I know that when you met again, in San Antonio, a few years later, he became your partner, here, at this ranch, until the treaty was signed at Fredericksburg, and he was offered a job there. I also know that it was there that he met Karin, and that he stayed there to be with her."

"Only after I convinced him that keeping peace was different, and more honorable, than making war. He died today, trying to do just that, to keep peace in the middle of this ungodly example. What right did I have to make that choice for him?"

"You didn't make a choice for him, Daniel. You only pointed out to him that he had one."

"Don't try to white-wash this fence, Maria. I know what I have done. Now, I must try to find out how I am to live with myself."

They laid Jake's body to rest a few days later and returned to the Double-R. Molly took the boys back to Fredericksburg, and to the house that she had lived in with Adam Sloane. Daniel was still in a very dark place. He went through the motions for Maria and the children, but all he could remember was what he said to Jake, that Easter fifteen years ago, when they went to Fredericksburg for the signing of the treaty with the Comanche, when Jake met Karin, and John Meusebach offered him the deputy's job. Jake had been set against it. Daniel had convinced him it was the right thing to do.

"Jake wanted a reason to stay in Fredericksburg, Daniel," Maria kept reminding him. "Karin was there. Her family had died trying to get there, and she believed it was her duty to stay and help to get the community on its feet," she continued to tell him these truths, but he could not hear her.

"And it didn't end there, my meddling. After Karin died, I convinced him to come to Sandy Creek. If he had stayed in Fredericksburg..."

"Fredericksburg is in the same situation as the rest of these hills, Daniel. Jake was Jake, and he would have taken the same stand now matter where he might have been." She had never seen this man she loved in such a low state of mind. She worried for him, and for all her family. She had to get him thinking about their future. "Chase and Molly said that the partisans told Jake that the conscription age had been raised to forty-five."

"And Lou Martin confirmed it."

"What will you do?"

"I can tell you what I won't do."

She knew what was coming, and the chill gripped her even stronger.

"I won't go to Fort Mason. I will not sign a loyalty oath, and I will not be conscripted."

She knew what that would mean as well.

"Maybe we should leave."

"And go where?"

"To the north, perhaps, or to Mexico, or..."

"Or what, Maria?"

"We could go to the caves."

He was silent for a while before he answered, "I have thought of that."

"And?"

"If we leave this land we will lose it. We cannot allow that to happen. And it isn't just about us. Your parents are not young, Maria. They need us, now. We have to look after them."

"It is true," she agreed, and found herself going into the dark with Daniel, but only for a little while. After a few minutes, her shoulders straightened and her dark eyes brightened. She turned to her husband and said, "So, you will have to go without us."

"What the hell does that mean?"

"You will go to the caves. The rest of us will move back to the *hacienda* with my parents."

"The hell I will. Maria, what are you thinking?"

"I don't think; I just know."

"Forget it."

Daniel, *mi esposo*, did you not promise me, before we wed, that I was to be your *compañera*, your equal?"

"You are more than my equal, Maria, but this idea is insane."

"This world is insane. Perhaps an insane answer will give us the means to survive in it."

"How?"

"If we both stay here, in our home, the partisans will come for you. If you do not give in to them, you will die as Jake died, and his death will truly be in vain."

He couldn't look at her. He closed his eyes and shook his head, trying to avoid seeing the reality of what she was saying.

"This time, you must trust me, *querido*."

"Don Tomas has always been one of the strongest men I know, but he is aging, and you know this."

"Yes, and so is Mama, and that is part of why this is the only way."

"And you have much of your father in you, love, but what you are suggesting is too much. It is enough that you must look after our house and children, to look after the work of the ranch - both ranches - you do not know what you would be getting yourself into."

"I know more than you think. Of course it will be difficult, but I will not be alone. You will have to be, but you will be alive, and, as you and Jake have been saying all along, the south cannot win this war. It *will* end, and we *will* be together again."

"You would be taking on too much."

"I will find a way..." She paused for a moment, thoughts running through her head more quickly than she could digest them. Then it started to fall in place. She spoke eagerly. "Molly and the boys will come with us. She has no family in Fredericksburg. She will be more than willing, I am sure if it."

Daniel looked at Maria then. He had never seen her quite this way.

"Molly is one of many widows having to cope with this war on her own. Please, Daniel, hear me, and don't make me one of them as well."

They made love on their last evening together for - they did not know how many - years, with a passionate intensity, filling each other with as much of themselves as they possibly could. They had been at the *hacienda* for over a week now. Molly, Chase, and Adam were settled into their own wing of the large main house. Dub and Maggie were enjoying being spoiled by *Abuelo* and *Abuelita*, and those same grandparents were happy to have them there for spoiling...at least while everyone adjusted. Don Tomas was pleased to have such an able *capataz* as Diego to run the *rancho* with him, and Isabela was overjoyed at having, not only her daughter, but a houseful of women to help her keep the household going. Maria had been working hard to keep everyone's spirits up, hiding from all of them her sadness over Daniel's coming departure. As for Daniel, he was still in that dark place, still feeling not only that he had contributed to the death of his closest friend, but that now he was failing his own family as well. He had reluctantly agreed that Maria's idea gave them a valid option; it did not keep him from feeling like he was running away...but run he finally did.

As soon as it was full dark and Diego had scouted to see that there were no partisans watching, he took the two strongest horses, one to ride, and the other to carry his small pack, and followed the same pathless route that he and Maria had taken on that night, ten years ago now, toward the grotto and through the narrow, hidden passageway into the hidden valley and the stone house where he and Maria had spent their honeymoon. Perhaps it was a good thing that he arrived there so exhausted, for he fell into a deep sleep, alone in that bed where they had their first night together.

When he woke the next morning, he busied himself with unpacking the few supplies he had brought. It did not take long enough. When it was done, he had nothing to do but think his own thoughts, and they were not pleasant thoughts. After a while, because there was nothing else to do, he entered the alcove at the back of the small house and opened the hidden door, descending to the caves below. He ached with Maria's absence, but he kept going, knowing where it was that he had to go, knowing that he had to get back to the hidden cave and that glowing red stone. As he grew closer, he could feel the talisman that still hung from the leather cord around his neck. It seemed to be growing warmer the closer he walked toward the hidden cavern.

And then he was there. It stood, in front of him, glowing as intensely as he remembered. He felt the penetration of its light throughout his body, and he dropped to his knees and wept.

It had begun with the soft roar of the wind in the rigging, the roll of the sea beneath his feet, and the endless stretch of the ocean in every direction. Then, he was at his childhood home again, walking beneath the tall pine trees and gigantic old oaks in the middle of a thick forest with no path to follow. He saw the deer, a great, old, many-horned stag, and he followed it. He could hear the sound of a rushing stream, and he walked toward it. The stream led him to a clearing, and a deep pool, fed by a narrow waterfall. He could smell smoke from a wood fire, and turned to see a large tipi. He walked over to it, and entered. A small fire burned in the center of the round dwelling, its flames glowing a golden red. He sat beside it and stared into the flames. He saw his grandmother's face, and then, his mother's. It had been many years since he had seen her, but he knew her right away, only there was a difference. The sad expression he remembered from his childhood, that permanent expression of lost hopelessness that had always been in the face of the woman he thought was his older sister, was gone, and she looked at him and smiled. As he continued to stare into the flames, he saw other faces, his father, looking much as he did just before Bandera Pass, but without the war paint. Karin Klemens Holder smiled warmly, and finally, he saw Jake, his broad hat tipped back, his eyes and face grinning beneath it, and then Jake's image grew more serious, and spoke to him, "We all did what we had to do, Daniel. Your mother, your father, Karin, and me. We made our choices, and did what had to be done, and Daniel," Jake's face loomed closer then, and his voice reverberated, "so did you. So, let it go, my friend. Let it go, and keep moving, keep following your path, wherever it leads you..." He heard another voice, then. Was it Jake's...or was it his own, echoing back to him from that Easter in Fredericksburg: *"Who is right in all this? Who is wrong?...And who gets to decide which is which?"*

He could still hear the sound of running water, and when he came back to himself, he was in the underground garden nearby the cavern with the red stone, and the water was sparkling, and running clear. He leaned toward it, cupped his hands, and drank deep.

Staying in the stone house was difficult. He missed Maria and the children, and the aloneness of his exile hit him harder there. He spent much of his time outside. The Penateka half of him was coming forward, but not the warrior so much as the hunter. He had brought his old Walker revolver, but only a limited supply of ammunition. He had the knife his father had given him, and with it, he fashioned a bow and some arrows from the hardwoods growing by the pond. On this particular day, he had ventured farther to the north and west than previously. He found himself drawn in that direction, and, before long, he was following an old, overgrown road that seemed familiar. It was though he had been in this place before, or one much like it. Some landmarks, he felt he knew, but there were as many more that seemed out of place. What intrigued him the most was the fence that he came cross a few miles up the road. It had wooden posts, but the rest of it was metal wire, and a strange wire, for every few feet along, it was wrapped with tiny, but very sharp, metal bits. It didn't take him long to figure their purpose. A horse or cow that might happen too close to it would get a painful, but relatively harmless prick. It would not take long before the animals realized that the fences should be avoided. They would be safely caged within its confines. It was only a mile or so beyond that that the road took on an even more familiar feel, and a breeze that stirred his hair gave him a shiver. He knew the rise ahead of him, he was sure of it, as he was sure of what he would find in the little valley beyond it. He rode more quickly, then, but as he reached the top of the ridge and looked down, he stopped the horse in its tracks. Below him, he saw what he had expected to see - the *hacienda* at Rancho Pineda, which he had left less than a week before, only now, it looked ancient: barren and deserted. The stone fence that had surrounded it had fallen from disuse, but as he continued to ride closer, he could see that the main house seemed solid. It had been built of stucco more than a hundred years earlier, by Don Tomas's ancestors, and it still looked as strong as ever, though neglected. Isabela's gardens were overgrown with weeds, and the weeds had spread over the stone walks and the patio. A few clay pots, mostly broken into fragments lay around the area. He slowly dismounted and walked to the door, which creaked open when he pushed. Once inside, he had no doubt where he was, it was clearly the same house, but empty. He continued to walk forward, slowly, compelled by a feeling he could not quite grasp. He walked past the *salon* and down the hall to the bedroom that had been Maria's, the same room where the two of them had slept together and made love for that last time before he rode away and entered the grotto that led to the stone house and the caves. He walked inside the empty room and looked around. The furniture, the large wardrobe, all of her things were gone, but as he closed his eyes, he could feel her presence, could even pick up a scent that he had come to cherish. It was as though she was present in the room, standing next to him.

Maria found her mother out in front of the main house, tending her gardens. Isabela leaned over and picked up a sizeable clay pot, filled with lavender, and very quickly set it down again. The daughter found herself scolding her mother. "Mama, be more careful of your back. You know better than to lift something so heavy."

"It needs more sun, *hijita*. But I have no objections if you care to help me."

"Of course I can help you." She moved over to the other side of the pot and asked, "Where do you wish it to be?"

"In the center of the herb garden, probably, what do you think?"

"I think you need to decide before we move it. It would be better not to have to lift it again."

Isabela ignored the crossness in her daughter's voice. It had only been a week since Daniel had left. She knew he had good reasons for going, but it still hurt to see her daughter taking on such responsibility.

"You have such a good eye for balance. Has the plant grown to enough of a size to be placed there, or would it be better in the corner near the gate?"

Maria worked to hide her annoyance. She understood that her mother was trying to help, but already, during the last few days, she had made more decisions than she would have made in more than a month, before this war had changed all of their lives. She sat back on her haunches and looked around. I think it is the perfect pot for the herb garden, Mama. Let's put it there."

Once the garden's pots were all in place, Maria excused herself and went inside, walking toward her old room. She needed to get away from all of them and their needs for a few minutes. When she reached her room, she went inside and closed the door. As soon as she did so, she started to feel something strange, like a familiar and beloved presence.

"Daniel?" She looked around the room, almost expecting to see him, the feeling was so strong.

Chapter 12

Daniel was reluctant to leave the deserted *hacienda*, but he had not planned to ride quite so far. Always before, when he had come into the hidden valley, he had stayed close to the stone house, mostly going underground, exploring the caves that connected it to the singing rock, but not venturing so far on the surface. Obviously, this other world place was also part of another time, but when? He had left his pack horse and supplies, and now felt his first priority was to get back to them. He had little trouble backtracking, but by the time he reached the house, it was almost dusk. He took time to finish dressing the game from his hunt, and stored the meat in the cold stone cavity above the underground spring. He shook his head in wonder at the simple technology that had been employed in the building of this little house. Its design hinted at a civilization that understood the importance of living with nature, rather than fighting to overcome it. He turned his attention back to his cache of food. He had spent some time foraging the afternoon before, and had found some onions and nettle plants. The crabapple trees were bearing, so he had picked some of the fruit, and tasting it, found that it was sweet enough to make a good addition to the stewed greens and onions he would cook to go with the meat.

He focused his attention on preparing his evening meal, letting the day's discoveries sit at the back of his mind, to digest later, along with his dinner.

He was almost ready to eat when he thought he heard a strange, faint sound. He stepped outside to listen more closely. Perhaps it was just the wind, playing tricks on him, but he thought he heard music. It came, or seemed to come, from far away, somewhere in the forest. Crickets, maybe, or night birds, but whatever it was seemed to carry more of a measured melody than the sounds of nature usually held. He turned back toward the house, and his meal. Hunger won out, but, just to be sure, he took his plate out to the porch, and sat on the bench to eat. The musical sounds did not end, so when he had eaten his fill, he lit a lantern and carried it with him toward the sound. With each step he grew more certain that someone, or something, was playing an instrument, a stringed instrument, maybe a guitar. He thought of the *vaqueros* sitting at night around the campfire of the cattle drives, playing softly to soothe the animals.

And then he saw the light - a campfire. He was not alone in this valley. He doused his own light, then, and continued to move cautiously ahead. The fire, he soon saw, was lit along the bank of a stream, in a small clearing in the forest, and the musician was a young man who looked to be in his early twenties. He sat on an old log, near the fire, playing a plaintive tune, and looking as though he carried the world on his shoulders. There was a horse, barely visible on the other side of clearing, and on the ground near the fire, a saddle and blankets for a bedroll. Daniel did not know whether to stay or go. He did not wish to make his presence known, but since he was obviously not the only human in the valley, and since he still had unanswered questions about the place, he decided to stay. The young man's hair was cropped quite short; he was wearing dark dungarees and a wool bolero jacket that looked as though it might have been made from a Penateka blanket. He reached inside the pocket of that jacket and pulled out a flask, opened it, and took a long drink. Daniel realized, at that point, that it was a long way from his first of the evening.

The man held the flask in his hand and stared into the fire in front of him, then looked up at the sky as though he was contemplating the stars, let out a deep sigh, and, in a voice tinged with both desperation and resignation asked, "Okay God, can you please tell me just what the hell I am supposed to do now?"

That point of sobriety somewhere at the back of the young musician's head was whispering above the bourbon fog that he ought to be cautious, but it was overwhelmed by curiosity directed at the apparition that seemed to be walking toward him from the darkness beyond his campfire. It looked to him like the ghost of a bearded Indian, but it seemed more benevolent than threatening, and since his aching loneliness hadn't been dissipated by the drink, he raised the flask and invited the apparition in.

"Welcome, Ghost," he said. "Come join in the celebration."

The ghost had a voice. It seemed friendly enough, even sounded more like an old-time Southern gentleman than a long-haired savage. "What are we celebrating?"

"My graduation." He passed his flask to the newcomer.

The ghost had walked in closer and had taken a seat on the ground, cross-legged. He accepted the flask and waved it under his nose. He smiled a little when he said, "Kentucky bourbon," then his eyes dimmed as he added in a sadder voice, "reminds me of an old friend." He took a short swig and handed the flask back, turning his attention to the younger man's statement.

"Graduated from?"

"Texas Agricultural and Mechanical University. Animal Husbandry." He raised the flask again before he took another drink. "Here's to the class of 1962." He smiled an ironic smile and finished, "Gig-em, Aggies."

The ghost took in a sharp breath and looked at the graduate with carefully veiled surprise. He reached for the bottle again and took a longer pull from it before asking, "*Nineteen* sixty-two?"

"September the...5th?"

"I guess. I've kind of lost track."

The guest was looking at the young man in an odd way. He seemed a little confused, like he wasn't sure he understood. It was beginning to sink in that this was not a vision or apparition, but an actual human being, if a strange one. He was dressed like one of the Indians in the Saturday morning westerns he had seen as a boy, only with a beard and blue eyes. He spoke like an educated man, but his questions indicated something different.

"Do you have a name, friend?"

"Dan...," the ghost-man hesitated, then finished, "Just call me Dan."

"Okay, just call me Johnny, then."

Dan reached out a hand.

Johnny shook it. There was something in Dan's eyes that told him it was okay to trust this curious stranger, something that he wanted to get to know better. Maybe in the morning, when he was sober, he would change his mind and regret the trust, but he did not think so.

Dan did seem to understand that Johnny was curious, but evaded any possible questions by saying, "So, Johnny, tell me more about yourself."

It had been a very long time since anyone had acted as though they really wanted to know about who he was, or how he felt. There was so much that he had been holding inside, for so long, that it all started to spill

111

out.

"I wasn't sure about the corps at first. A&M has the best program for learning modern techniques for farming and ranching, and I just assumed, along with my dad, that it was what I would do. I didn't think that much, at the time, about whether it was okay to take advantage of family connections so that I could go into active reserve quickly. It kept me from worrying about getting drafted as soon as I finished school, and that was the important thing. At least that's what I thought then."

Dan was watching Johnny intently, listening carefully to each word. His eyes had quickened when Johnny spoke of the draft. He prodded a little by asking, "You changed your mind about the...corps?"

"I didn't expect to get into it so much: The discipline, the training. I was good at it, too. It gave me a lot of confidence - in myself. My dad is a pretty strong individual. It wasn't until I got away from home, living with other guys my own age, studying, that I thought I might want something different for myself. I liked the classes, too. It isn't that ranching would be a bad career, it's just that being a soldier, especially an officer, feels...right...for me, like it's what I am supposed to do."

Daniel poured himself a cup of coffee and took it out to the small porch. The sun was already high. He had not slept well. After saying good-night to young Johnny, and walking back to the house, he found his mind so awash with what he had learned that it took most of the night to digest it all.

He started to count back the days since his arrival. If his recollections were accurate, he had, to the day, moved ahead in time by precisely a century...one hundred years ahead of where, or rather when, he was supposed to be.

He had been careful to let this Johnny do most of the talking. It had taken him awhile to adjust to the young man's manner of speaking, as well as to figure out some of the words, words that were not unknown to him as much as they were being used in an unfamiliar context. He sipped his coffee and reflected on what he had learned. So, he thought, in a hundred years, young men would be getting college degrees in farming and ranching. They would have the option of obtaining military officer's training while attending classes, and in some cases, be able to pursue their own choice of civilian careers afterward, by agreeing to attend regular training sessions, and to promise to return to active duty in case there was a war. *In case there was a war.* He allowed that to sink in. Texas, he had also learned, was once again a state, one of the United States. The south had lost the war as he had predicted. Slavery had been abolished, and the southern states were finally becoming a part of the industrialized world. So far, so good, but he worried about the particulars. The Pineda hacienda had been abandoned. What had happened to the Double-R? And the most important thing: What had happened to his family?

He set his cup aside and stood, then walked in the direction of the campsite he had been to the night before. He was curious about something. There had been a point, during his walk back, when he thought he was lost. It hadn't panicked him. He remembered the times in his youth, when he had come to this place and to the caves underneath. There would be moments when he had not known where to go next, but he would stop, relax and refocus, and something would always appear to stand out that indicated the direction he needed to take. That sense had come back to him more than once over the last week or so. It had been especially strong when he was returning from the deserted *hacienda.* As he walked toward the edge of the clearing, and into the trees, he felt it again. After a few yards, he turned to look back, and once again, had a momentary sense of being lost. He looked around more carefully, then walked in the direction that seemed to stand out, and was soon back where he had started. That was it, he thought to himself, this place: including the clearing, the pond, and the stone house, was a protected place. Just as he had learned all those years earlier, whenever he had tried to find it from his own world, it did not seem to exist. It was like a gateway, a door, into a different time. If he were to retrace his passage through the opening in the cliffs, as he had done so often before, he would come out in the grotto, and into his own time and place, but if he left through the trees - as he had the night before, and earlier, as he was hunting, and came upon the *hacienda* - he was in a different world, at least as far as time was concerned.

He was glad he had told Johnny he would return. The young man was troubled about his future, and had chosen to take a solitary journey into the hills, to spend some time alone, in an effort to make up his mind. Daniel understood his dilemma. He knew what it was like to have to choose between two ways of living, both desirable but mutually exclusive. Maybe he could just listen to Johnny, and give him an objective source to hear his thoughts as he struggled to make his choices. Daniel's grandmother had been such a source for him, when he was about Johnny's age. It would be a good way to adjust to this limbo he was living in, and a means of learning more, if he could, about the past hundred years, and what had become of his own family.

Johnny was glad that Dan had kept his word, and had come back the next day, especially as he had arrived with a freshly dressed pheasant in one hand, and a bow in the other, a quiver of arrows slung across his back. They sat and talked together as Dan rigged a spit for roasting the bird, and washed some berries and wild onions. His head was a lot clearer now. It had ached for several hours after he had awakened that morning. Getting drunk had done nothing to solve his problem, but being found by this strange man was putting him in a more hopeful mood.

"Man, that bird smells good. And I thought I was in for another day of Spam."

"Spam?"

"You don't even want to know."

"I can tell by the sound of the word. It doesn't sound like any animal I ever heard of." He turned his attention from the bird to the small iron pot that sat on a stone near the edge of the fire, and added some onions to the simmering berries. "I often wonder if it was not a mistake when people settled into growing their own crops instead of picking whatever they found along the hunting trails."

"Or herding their livestock instead of following them around?"

"That, too." Dan had a funny way of crinkling his eyes when something amused him.

From what Johnny had seen so far, it didn't happen that often. Dan didn't talk about himself, or what he was doing living out in the wild parts of these hills. And even though he asked intelligent questions, it was clear that he didn't actually know very much, at least about the world they both apparently lived in.

"You don't care much for civilization, do you?"

"I try to avoid it, when I can," Dan even laughed then.

"You dress and act like an Indian, but you're as white as I am."

"Maybe not. My father was Comanche."

"Shit. They say that the Comanche were the most bloodthirsty tribe of all. I guess it's a good thing I don't have much of a scalp." He ran a hand across his burr-cut head and laughed.

Dan took his words in the spirit he had meant them, and laughed back. "Could be, but long hair was a warrior's sign of honor, sort of like a dare for his enemies. Cutting it off was not exactly a sign of bravery."

"Hell, not true in today's Army. Not anywhere around here. While I was still in high school, I tried letting it grow a little, but whenever it got long enough to start to curl against my neck, my dad sent me to the barber."

"So, who is this 'they' you spoke of?"

Johnny shrugged, "Teachers, I guess. Books; movies."

"Movies?"

"Films; motion pictures. You've never been to a theater?"

"Not in a long time," Dan said wryly, and added, "They were never a tribe, you know. The Comanche. Each band is independent of the others. Each has its own leaders."

"Your father taught you their history?"

"My father, yes, and my grandmother. Mostly my grandmother."

Johnny noticed that Dan always measured his words carefully. "Did you live in Oklahoma?"

Dan gave him a questioning glance.

"On the reservation, I mean."

"No. I've lived most of my life in these hills."

"Which part?"

"Around." He had said as much about himself as he was going to say, and turned the conversation bake onto the younger man. "How about you? Have you lived here always?"

"Longer than always, I guess. The Double-R has belonged to my family since there were Americans in Texas."

It came as something of a surprise to Stone, one afternoon, that he had, somewhere along the way, become perfectly comfortable sitting on the back of a horse.

He had been out riding with Dan, getting to know more about the hills of this place he was starting to call home. They were riding in a remote area to the northeast of Sandy Creek, near the end of the La Roca County line, in a secluded pocket of land that was still as wild as it must have been when the first settlers had arrived, almost two hundred years earlier, and he was thinking about how necessary this business of riding and tracking was to his new job, here in this part of the world where Nature was still a force to be reckoned with. They were climbing toward the top of a high ridge. There was no trail, and the rocks and boulders had huge clumps of prickly pear cactus growing between them. As they approached the top, Stone looked back. He could see a narrow dirt road winding below them, the only sign that they were anywhere close to civilization, and yet, he knew that they weren't more than five or six miles from town. Another few yards and they reached the top, and turned around to look southwest. He could easily see Granite Hill, and as he looked even farther into the distance, an amazing view of the whole north face of The Rock.

"Do you ever get used to it?"

"The impact? I haven't, and I've been looking at it for more years than I like to think about."

Stone could not help but wonder about Dan's age. The man's white hair and beard and the deep lines around his eyes said one thing; his strength and the firm leanness of his body said another, but he decided it was none of his business, so he kept silent.

"You hungry? Dan asked.

"I'm okay."

"You sure? I'm pretty damned hungry, myself."

"You got something to eat? I could eat."

"Why don't we ride back down toward the creek and I'll see what I've got."

Stone had come to know Dan well enough to know that whatever the man packed in his saddlebags was generally a lot more than hardtack and jerky. He was more than willing to find out what it might be, this trip.

They found a spot near the northernmost point of the creek and started a fire. Dan moved a couple of flat rocks close to the flames, and headed for a patch of prickly pear, pulled an old, but clearly sharp knife and cut off a few of the smaller of the spiny, thick leaves that looked like a cross between porcupines and ping-pong paddles. When he reached into his bags again and brought out a pair of needle-nose pliers, he most

116

definitely had Stone's attention. Dan used them to pull out the spines, then he washed the paddles and placed them on the hot stones. While the paddles sizzled, he brought out a package of corn tortillas, a small block of crumbly cojito – a Mexican version of feta cheese - and some sticks of dried sausage.

Stone knew what they were. "Chorizo," he said, voicing a high degree of pleasure.

"Spanish chorizo," Dan nodded. Mexican chorizo was a soft, uncooked sausage link that looked a bit like Italian sausage, but with a distinctively different seasoning. Spanish chorizo was closer to a hard salami or pepperoni, but, again, with its own distinctive taste. Dan cut it into paper thin slices. He tossed some of tortillas onto the other stones, and sprinkled them with the slices of sausage and crumbly cheese. He turned the cactus paddles and let them brown on their other side before he sliced them into thin strips. In the meantime, Stone took their canteens over to the creek and filled them with fresh, cool water. They sat in the shade, then, munching away on their rolled cactus and chorizo tacos, not saying much of anything, just getting lost in the pleasure of the early afternoon.

After a while, Dan asked him, "So, what really brought you to this quiet countryside after living in such a big city?"

Somewhere at the back of his head, he had the feeling that, somehow or another, Dan already knew, and had even set this whole situation up so that he had the opportunity to ask the question, but Stone also knew that he wanted to tell the old man, and for some reason, for the first time, the words spilled out easily, even as he got to the end. "I stayed on the job for over a year, but I was going through the motions. Then the captain called me in and told about an old Army buddy – this guy from Texas who had served with him in 'Nam – who was looking for a deputy. I knew I had to take the offer, for the kids if not for myself. It's proving to be a good move. I already feel more at home here than I ever did in Jersey, or in the city, but I still can't get beyond what happened to Erin. Shit, when I even start to think that maybe I could, I'm right back in my hole. Khani thinks I'm being too hard on myself. Sometimes I want to believe her, but most of the time I don't think I'm being hard enough. My wife is dead because I screwed up. How do I reconcile that?"

Dan took a minute to make sure the last of their fire was out before he replied, "Remember the story of Atlas?"

"Atlas, as in the god?"

117

"The Greek Titan who carried the world on his shoulders, yes; that god."

I remember him more from Rand's book.

"*Atlas Shrugged*. What did you think of it?"

"I'm a cop. I don't make the laws and I don't get to choose which ones ought to be enforced. That was my mistake that day. I chose not to enforce a law, and now I have to live with myself and the consequences of that choice. So I don't go along with the idea of breaking or ignoring an unjust law. On the other hand, I agree with her view of objective reality, and in relying on logic as the basis for making choices. I screwed up there, too."

"Ever think that maybe 'the heart has its own reasons'?"

"That reason doesn't know about. Who was that? I've heard it, but I can't remember where."

"Pascal."

"Shit, Dan. Is there anybody you haven't read?"

"I'm an old man. One of the good things about that is having time to read more than the *Sandy Creek Gazette*," then he looked at Stone with that crinkle growing around his eyes as he added, "or the *New York Times*." But the more I read philosophy, the more I get a sense of humanity running back and forth between extremes. That's what I like about living close to Nature. The concept of either/or just isn't part of Her vocabulary. She doesn't get hung up over what is right or wrong." He looked at Stone directly as he got back to his original point. "Atlas was a god, so maybe carrying the world on his shoulders was his job, and something he had to live with, but men are not gods, son." He looked even more directly into the younger man's eyes, and in a quietly gentle but firm voice added, "It's when we get the notion that we ought to have that kind of power that we screw up."

If that had come from anyone but Dan, Stone would probably have taken offence. Instead, he just listened as the old man explained.

"We all make choices; that's a given. You were not the only one making a choice that day. Your partner chose to go along. Those kids chose to get high, and then they chose to take that car, drive it, and to attempt to evade the police car. The officer driving that car chose to try and stop them. Even your wife made the choice to go into the city that day, and all of those coincidental choices contributed to the pile-up on the freeway. That's how Nature works, like ripples in a pond that come in contact with other ripples, or the way that forces in a storm cloud might cause a whirlwind, and that whirlwind follows its own path, which just might include a house or even a school on a busy school day. The whirlwind isn't evil; it isn't even wrong; it's just doing what it is supposed to do." Dan stopped talking for a minute, giving Stone time to listen before he continued. "We make our choices based on the best knowledge we have available at the time. Sometimes the result is not what we would have wished, because no one of us is ever the only factor involved, and all of our perspectives are limited." He paused once more before he finished. "You carry that kind of load, Josh, it's like playing god. It's okay to put it down, or just let it go. In fact, it's the right thing to do."

Chapter 13

Over the next months, Daniel made several trips to the clearing where he had met Johnny. One day, as he walked into the clearing had become their meeting place, Johnny was already preparing a meal. "I had a feeling you would come around today. Last night I made a trip back to the house for something special."

"Is there an occasion?"

"A last one, I guess. At least for a good while." He took a minute to pick up an iron grate from the ground, and set over the stones around the fire, then sat back on his haunches and looked at Daniel. "I told my father that I was volunteering for active duty, and that I would probably be leaving soon for Fort Bragg."

"Fort Bragg?"

"North Carolina. Helicopter training."

Daniel knew, now, what a helicopter was. He had been listening to Johnny over the past months. He knew that technology had gone beyond steam engines and trains to motors that ran on a combustible fuel called gasoline, that the young man was planning to trade in his "old dodge" for a newly developed "mustang," which wasn't a horse, but a "car," which ran on this fuel, and could travel over a hundred miles an hour. He had seen the excitement in Johnny's eyes when he talked about such things. That same excitement was in his eyes now, as he told Daniel of his plans to become an active duty Army officer. "How did your father take your news?"

"Not good. He thinks I'm deserting the family and shirking my responsibilities here."

Daniel understood something of Johnny's pain. He had felt it himself when he left the Penateka, but he knew that his father would have given his blessing, if he had still been alive. How much harder it must be for this young man. Daniel also knew, from first-hand experience, what a terrible thing war was, what it could do to a man. He knew, through Jake, what it took to commit your life to defending ordinary citizens from those who would do them harm. He had convinced Jake that there was a difference between making war and keeping peace, but he had learned that the differences were not so well defined. And right now, listening to this young man, he also knew, finally, for certain, that a man must follow his calling, whatever it might be. He knew what his answer to Johnny had to

120

be. "Your only responsibility, son," he told this young man whom he guessed might very well be his own descendant, "is to follow your heart. Only you can know what that is. Do whatever it is that you believe you have to do."

Johnny nodded, grateful to have a friend who understood. "In the meantime, I haven't left yet." He reached into his pack and brought out a package wrapped in brown paper. "Prime beef steaks from a Double-R steer." Next he pulled out two oval packages, wrapped in what looked like a paper-thin metal. "Partly cooked potatoes, so they will finish with the steaks, and for when they are done," he then pulled out a brown paper bag, which looked to be filled with greens of some kind, "a salad from my mom's garden." Then he opened the strange looking white chest that was sitting near him, which was filled with ice that had been crushed, and several brown glass bottles sitting in the ice. "Hope you like Lone Star."

Maria walked from the *cocina* back to the main house. It seemed to be working out, she thought to herself. Her mother was content to oversee the kitchen and gardens, and seemed relieved to have Maria looking after the rest of the household. Diego and her father had a growing mutual respect, and between Molly and Lucia, they were able to take care of things without anyone being too overworked. Not that Maria minded working. It kept her from thinking too much, and it made the days go faster. She did not want to count the time. No one knew when the war would end, although it did seem more and more likely that the south would lose. She had to be careful about saying so, at least out loud. They had been visited more than once by the partisan companies. Captain Duff had been replaced by a Major Hunter, who had seemed more reasonable, but as the war had entered yet another year, the conscription orders were being pushed even harder. Adam and Chase would both soon turn fifteen, and they looked older, especially Chase, who was now almost as tall as his father had been. Whenever the partisans came, they would remind Molly that her husband had died a "traitor," and would point out to Maria that her husband, who had since deserted her and his family, had been a close friend to Jake. It was so hard for her to keep quiet at those times. For everyone's sake, she dared not say anything that could give the impression that Daniel was still in the valley.

She knew that he was. There were times, like today, when she could feel his presence. Sometimes, especially in her own rooms, the feeling was so intense she expected to turn and see him. There were other times, though, at least as often, that she could not, no matter how she tried, get quite that same sensation of his closeness. She would close her eyes and remember back to their honeymoon, and the small stone house on the other side of the grotto. The rest of it, the caves, and where they led, she actively worked to keep out of her conscious memory, in case the worst should happen and she was arrested. It would not be the first time. The partisans would often arrest the families of the "traitors," as they called them. Thank God for her father and his presence. He was so cool with the rangers. They were intimidated by him, and did little more than harass the *hacienda* with empty threats. She found herself shuddering a little, and was glad that today was one of the days that Daniel seemed near.

Daniel sometimes wondered if he should move his home base to here, at the *hacienda*. When he was here, he felt as though he could almost reach out and touch Maria. But when he was being rational, he knew that it was unprotected, even though deserted and remote. As time had passed, he had seen more and more of this twentieth century, especially here in this valley. He had seen cattle with the Double-R brand, now that the weather was growing warmer again, and the herds were being moved into summer grass. They were a strange breed, with short horns and dark red-brown coats. They were fat, like the steaks Johnny had cooked at their last dinner. Instead of being driven to market, he had learned, they were loaded onto gigantic trucks, fed by the same fuel that fed Johnny's "old dodge." And he had even seen them, lumbering along the hard, dark roadways that connected the towns. He had even ventured into his own Sandy Creek, and found a corner where men older than he in terms of years, gathered to talk about the old times. He had learned from them the time of the war's end, and now he knew he could count down the days. But he had also learned that he had to be careful.

It was not just that he might be discovered, or even followed back to the hidden cabin with its secrets, although that was a danger. It also came from an understanding that he must not learn any more than was necessary of this time, and especially of his family's place in it. He needed to know enough to get safely home at the right time. Beyond that, the responsibility would be too great. He was coming, more all the time, to a grasp of the importance of letting life unfold as it was meant to unfold, and that the reasons for its development were beyond human understanding. He was becoming even more certain that there was a power greater than man could know or understand, and that the power of the red stone, hidden in the caves and caverns below, was a part of it all. He could understand, too, the temptation one might have to attempt to harness that power, to bring it under control and use it to selfish ends. He understood more than ever his grandmother's admonitions, and why, as the stone's keeper he needed to protect it from such misuse. So he stayed away from the civilized places, especially from his own Double-R, and kept to the old trails where he would not likely be noticed, but he could not bring himself to stay away from the *hacienda*, for he knew, from being there, that his Maria was there, too.

He slept in her room that night. It was a deep and peaceful sleep. He hoped that Maria had slept so soundly as well. When he awoke, he went outside, and walked around the grounds. He found himself at the old Pineda family cemetery. He had been here before, but this time, as he approached, he felt an unexplainable apprehension, and as he looked closer, he realized there was a new stone. Not new in the sense of being fresh, for it had the same worn look as the others, but he was sure that it had not been there before. He walked over to it, feeling a strong trepidation, and looked down. It read, "Tomas Antonio de Pineda y Perez; 1797 - 1864."

Chase Holder rode cautiously through the fields of dry grass, cactus, and mesquite, looking for signs of Dub and Adam, who had ridden out together the morning before to check on the herd of mustangs that were grazing in this part of the hills around the *rancho*. Neither of the boys had come home, so as soon as it was light, he, Diego, and Don Tomas had ridden out to find them. He did not want to think about what might have happened. Word had got out that the new leader of the Partisan Rangers, a local named William Banta, had joined forces with a group of Quantrill's Raiders, down from Missouri to buy stock and supplies, and they were raiding the settlers in the area, especially those who were rumored to be Union supporters. Innocent men had been arrested, whipped, even hung - lynched was the word, since there was never a trial. Governor Lubbock and Colonel McCullough had declared martial law in the area, and it had given Banta the means to attack, slash and burn, whether he had cause or not. Soon, Chase heard two pistol shots. It was the signal each of them had agreed to use to summon the others. He rode over the next ridge, and was headed into a wooded valley when he saw a group of men in a clearing. He slowed down, but continued riding carefully toward the group. He could see Dub and Adam on the ground, kneeling. The other men, most of them on horseback, lined up in two groups, facing each other. He recognized Don Tomas and Diego as the leaders of one group. The men on the other side were strangers to him, although he did notice that a couple of them wore guerilla shirts, the long, red wool overshirts that were the mark of the Missouri men who rode with William Quantrill. He rode closer and lined up with Don Tomas and Diego. Don Tomas was talking to the apparent leaders of the other group.

"You have no papers to show why you have taken these boys, and no witnesses to what you say they may have done."

"We don't need papers. We know well enough that you are harboring abolitionists. We know that these two haven't registered."

"They are not yet sixteen."

"How about this'n?" One of the men pointed his gun at Chase.

"My name is Chase Holder. I am fifteen years old. That one," he indicated Adam, "is my step-brother, and the other one, nodding towards Dub, is Don Tomas's grandson. Neither of them has turned sixteen, and this land is part of *El Rancho de Pineda*, and has been for more than a century."

"From a Spanish land grant," added Don Tomas.

"That don't mean nothing..."

"I assure you that it does, Captain Banta, and you know this is true, since you have lived in these hills since Texas was a Republic."

Chase stood his ground with the others. *So that is William Banta*, he thought to himself. Don Tomas might be getting older. His white hair and beard were signs of that, but the man was still strong enough to make his stand, and Chase was proud to be standing with him.

"So, Captain," the old man repeated firmly, "unless you have papers, and proof, I insist that you release these boys and leave my land. If not, Colonel McCullough will know of it. You have my word."

The captain reluctantly motioned his men away.

Chase dismounted, drew a knife, and cut the ropes binding the boy's hands. When he did so, he could see the red-tinged slashes in the back of Adam's shirt. He turned Dub's shoulder, then, and saw similar marks on his back as well.

"What happened?"

Dub spoke first. "They tried to get us to tell them where Papa was. But don't worry. It wouldn't have worked, even if we'd known."

"Adam?"

"Yeah, they had a bullwhip, but don't worry; we'll live," Adam replied bitterly.

The house was quiet that evening. Maria and Molly had washed and dressed their boys' cuts. Isabela and Lucia served dinner, and after, Chase, Diego, and Tomas took turns watching the windows. Maggie sat quietly as well, unusually subdued. All of them felt the tension. This war had come home to the hacienda, and no one knew what to say.

The first thing they heard was the whoosh of the flame, then the screams of the animals, and after, gunfire, and the sound of the horses hooves as they were stampeded away. Don Tomas was the first out the door. As he ran toward the burning barn, the two men in guerilla shirts fired toward him, and he fell. Chase and Adam fired after them, but Diego called for them to help him get as many of the animals as they could away from the barn. Maria ran to her father, but she saw immediately that he was beyond her help. Isabela held him, sobbing, while Molly stood, helpless to do anything except clench her fists. Maggie looked on all of it, clutching herself tightly, refusing to allow herself to cry.

Maria wrapped the loose end of the lariat around the horn of her saddle and backed her horse so that the rope stayed taut, as Daniel had shown her shortly after they married, while Chase wrestled the calf to the ground and held it as Dub burned the Double-R brand into its side. She had ridden with her husband often during those early days, even for a time after she was carrying Dub, once Lucia had convinced Daniel it was okay.

It hadn't taken long for those skills to return. Isabela still tended the gardens and cooked, though much of the life had gone out of her. If it hadn't been for the large household, she might have given up, but they gave her reason to keep going. Molly, with Lucia's help, looked after the rest of the household, and kept the children at their lessons. Adam and Chase thought they ought to be allowed to work full time, but she kept them reined in as well, for a few hours at least, reading and discussing the books from the library that the families had put together. She steeped them in Wordsworth and Goethe and even Victor Hugo, working in her special way to instill a love of idealism in them, in spite of the harsh realities of living through a war. Maggie had come through that horrible night, and was developing a resilience, an inner strength and even wisdom that was unusual for a ten-year-old.

Most of their horses were gone, in Missouri by now, with the raiders who had murdered Don Tomas. They hung on to as many of the cattle as they could, branding their own calves as well as a fair share of the strays that wandered the hills around Rancho Pineda and the Double-R. There were no easy days, but they all kept going, encouraged by the news that the Confederacy was losing ground, and believing that the war could not carry on much longer.

After the death of Don Tomas, and of several other men of the hills, from the depredations of the raiders, Colonel McCullough finally called them off, so the boys were relatively safe, as long as they stuck to their work and kept quiet.

Maria took a moment to look around. She could not help but feel pleased. The children were growing, the boys, almost men now. The sun was bright, the breeze was growing warmer, and the first of the spring wildflowers were cropping up, especially around the cactus plants and in the crevices of the limestone and granite rocks. She could see *La Roca Encantada*, off, far in the distance, rising above the landscape, singing a song of peace, singing a promise: *Daniel will be home soon.*

Chapter 14

Johnny rode into the grove of oak trees, pulled up, and dismounted. He walked over to the small circle of stones that was the only thing left of the fire pit where he had sat and talked with his mysterious friend. It was over a year, now, since he had told the man he was heading for North Carolina and Fort Bragg. He shifted his shoulders a little, and rocked into the toes of his western boots. Odd how uncomfortable these old clothes felt. He had become used to wearing a uniform. The denim jeans that had always been so comfortable now seemed loose and slouchy. He sat on the old fallen log and stared into the fire pit. He hadn't really expected that Dan might be here. It just seemed the right thing to do, anyway, to come here and tell him what was happening. He had the feeling that Dan might somehow know, even if they didn't actually meet to talk about it. He sat there, not saying anything, thinking very little, and then, he couldn't help but laugh.

Dan had a quiet way of walking. From the earliest of their visits, he could almost feel him before he could see him. He didn't even look up this time. "I had a feeling you might show up."

Dan squatted, as he always had, and sat on the ground, close to the fire pit. "You were almost wrong." He wasn't quite smiling, but that crinkle around his eyes was there. "I've been packing up. I was about ready to ride out when something told me I should make one last stop."

"Where are you headed?"

"Home. It's time. What brings you back?"

"I got a weekend pass. When I get back, I'll be shipping out. I wanted to say goodbye, to my folks, and to you."

"Shipping out."

"I'm on my way to Vietnam. He had learned to accept that this hermit, for whatever reason, did not know much about what was going on in the rest of the world, so he explained. "It's on the other side of the world from here. There is a war going on, between the north and south sections of the country, and *our* country is about to get involved."

"There is always a war going on somewhere, I suppose. What makes this one important enough to go such a distance?"

Johnny was quiet for a moment, trying to decide how to explain. "The last big war, my dad's war, went worldwide because people waited too long, and a sick idea was allowed to spread to the point where civilization itself might have been destroyed, if the notion wasn't stopped."

"A sick notion?"

"An elitist notion, a belief that a powerful few had the right to take over, to dominate and control, and to force the rest of the people into submission, taking away the concept of freedom, and a man's right to choose. The right side won that war, but in order to win, they unleashed a technology that threatens to destroy the world itself. If that technology gets into the wrong hands..." Johnny shook his head. "Well, it's just unthinkable. So now, we are stuck with doing what we can to keep that from happening. If the wrong side of the civil war going on in this little divided country should win..." He just opened his hands in a gesture of futility. He shifted directions and spoke of his present situation. "My dad is pissed. He was upset when I decided to go into active service, now he's saying that this is the reason. Upset is no longer the word for it. He's pretty much turned his back. It doesn't look like there will ever be a way to fix things."

Daniel just closed his eyes. A part of him wanted to tell this young man that war was never a proper answer, but another part wondered if that was so, and another, deeper part cautioned him that it was not his decision to make, that what Johnny needed from him was assurance. "You still have to follow your heart, Johnny," was all he said.

"Dan?"

"I'm right here, son."

"Were you ever in a battle? I mean a real one, where just staying alive was a question."

"More than once, yes."

"Were you scared?"

"Shitless. When you aren't afraid - that's when you need to start worrying. A man who isn't afraid can get a lot of people needlessly killed." He stopped a little while to get his next thoughts in place, then said, "John," Johnny just didn't seem to fit any longer, "I think we have come to know each other pretty well. And what I know about you is that you are a man of honor, and of courage, which isn't about being unafraid, it's about going on in spite of being afraid, and doing what you know needs to be done. Trust yourself. That's the best advice I can give you."

The wildflowers were in full bloom, now. The hills just outside the *hacienda* were brilliant with color. Isabela's herb garden had never been so fragrant. Chase, Adam, and Dub had ridden off to help Diego with the spring round-up, and Maggie was in the *cocina* with the rest of the women. Maria was enjoying a moment of solitude. She took a deep breath and let the scents of her mother's garden fill her head. Most of the time, taking a walk here was her way of relaxing, but not today. She could not shake off a feeling of excitement. Diego had come back from a trip down to Sandy Creek, and returned with rumors that the war was ending. Peace had been declared in the east, people were saying, and it would only be a matter of time before the armies here would be disbanded.

Maria believed the rumors. For days now, Daniel's presence had been strong and reassuring. She had come to trust in that presence. Many times over the past three years since he had left, she had felt that he was close, and this morning the feeling was stronger than ever. She found herself watching the ridge of hills that ran southeast of the main house. It was in that direction, that she and Daniel had fled, all those years ago that seemed like yesterday, when he took her into the hidden valley, and she truly became his wife. Something told her that if she looked long enough, and closely enough, she would see him, riding toward her through the bluebonnets and blazing reds and yellows of paintbrush and tickseed. She wished it so strongly that he seemed to appear. It was as though he had come up over the top of the ridge and was riding hard toward her. It took a while for her to realize that it was not an apparition. Once it sunk in that she was truly seeing him, she ran from the yard toward the ridge, watching as he came closer and closer. And then he was off his horse, and picking her up, and the strong arms that she had missed so were truly holding her, and then they were rolling on the ground, in the flowers, laughing and crying and drowning each other with kisses.

Later, when they had finally been able to retreat from the hugs and the questions to the privacy of her rooms, they were at last free to allow the pent-up passions that they had been holding in for the last three years to be released, and when they were finally spent, they continued to hold each other, tightly, both of their faces wet from the tears of the other.

Neither of them could sleep; neither wanted to risk waking up to the possibility that this was a dream, so they spoke together, softly. Maria wanted for Daniel to do most of the talking. There would be time for recounting the troubles. She wanted to know of the hidden valley, and how he had spent his time there. He told her of finding the hacienda, deserted, but also that he could feel her presence whenever he was there, and how it kept him going.

"But, I wasn't completely alone." He lay on his side, facing her, his head propped by one hand while the other kept touching her, running fingers through her hair, stroking her shoulder, as if to remind himself that she was real. He told her, then, about Johnny, and how he learned from the young man that he had entered the future. He told her how he learned that the war would end, and when it would end, and how. He told her how he came to believe that this young man was probably their descendant, and of his decision to learn as little as possible about that future world, so that when he returned he would be as free of its influences as possible. "I guess, what I mostly learned from Johnny was an affirmation that power, in and of itself, is not right or wrong, that it's more about how it is used, and who controls that use."

Maria reached her hand up to the medallion he still wore around his neck, and held it. "And we did what we had to do, *querida*, and we will continue to do so."

He lowered his head to kiss her, gently, and pulled her into his arms, and at last, they fell into a peaceful sleep.

"The horses are mostly gone, probably all the way to Missouri, but we've been able to keep track of enough of the cattle to keep the spread going. There isn't much of a market, at least there hasn't been. That might change now." Chase and Daniel had been riding south, toward the Double-R, as the young man explained what had been happening while the older man had been away. "The house itself is in pretty good shape. We've used it as a base camp for winter grazing, and made sure the Double-R itself was occupied and in use. Don Tomas wanted to make sure there were no claims against the property, and we've stuck to his plan since the raid."

As Daniel listened to the young man who rode beside him, he

remembered Maria's words from the night before: "After Papa died, he just took over. He became our strength." Daniel could see that strength in Chase right now, both emotionally and physically.

His voice had deepened, and he spoke with a conviction that fit well with the broad shoulders and straight back. "We had some good rain during the winter. Not much snow, and most of that in the north range. We moved the herd back up there last month. The grass was already green and thick. We'll have more than a few new calves when we start the round-up."

"You've done a good job, Chase."

The younger man smiled a little and shook his head, "Don Tomas was one wise old man. All we've done is carry on. Diego knows his way around a cow, too." Chase had a way of looking at a man eye to eye. It reminded Daniel of Jake. "After the raid on Rancho Pineda, Henry McCullough finally got off his ass and clamped down on the partisans. They left us pretty much alone, then. By the time Adam and I turned sixteen, there was nobody around to force conscription on us, and we were able to concentrate on the work here."

"I should have been here."

"Bullshit. You would have been as dead as my father. You did the right thing. It's done now, and Dub and Maggie won't have to grow up without you around."

"Not any more, anyway. I will see to that."

"And I'll be here to help with that, Uncle, as long as you will let me be."

"Then prepare to settle in, son, because you are an important part of this operation. Your father and I built this place up together. The way I see it, you are as much a member of the family as Dub and Maggie. And that includes Molly and Adam, too."

They crossed the creek a mile later. Daniel was officially back on his Double-R. After another few miles, he could see his home. Chase had been right about the house. It was sound, and after a bit of clean-up, it would be inhabitable again. The barn had been ransacked, and had quite a few boards missing. The corral was gone. "It looks like we will be staying at the *hacienda* a while longer." Daniel tried not to think about the deserted rancho he had seen in that future world he had been inhabiting. "You, Adam, and your mother will need more space, another house, or a wing built on to this one."

It was clearly something Chase had thought about already. "You and Pa built the house strong. It has good lines. We could close in the dog-trot and the back veranda. That would add some living space, and the women could have a modern kitchen to work in. Diego and Lucia would have a full-sized house, then, by taking in the old kitchen. A couple of wings on either side of the house..."

Daniel smiled. Chase's voice had more excitement in it than he had heard since coming home. The young man's eyes had a sparkle to them that matched the voice.

"...Sorry. I didn't mean to push. It's just...I've been coming back here whenever I got the chance. Mostly to see the rock, I guess. I don't know why, but seeing it kept me going, especially in the beginning. I would sit on the front steps and just watch it. You and Pa picked just the right spot to build. It isn't my place to say, but I can see a fine ranch house, with that view, and it's a lot closer to Sandy Creek than the *hacienda*." He stopped, looked a little embarrassed, and shrugged.

"I can see it too, Chase, thanks to your description. I believe you are right. It would be better to add to this house than it would be to build another."

"I don't think it would take much convincing for Abuelita Isabela to leave the *hacienda*, now that Don Tomas is gone. We could still use the north range in the summer, but the Double-R, it seems to me, would be the better place to live." He looked embarrassed again. "Besides, I like the idea of building things."

"And I like your ideas, Chase. Tell me more about what you see for this house."

Stone and Khani sat together in the overstuffed chair at the corner of the wide veranda that surrounded the guest house, and watched the sun set over the rock. "This is some guest house," he said, looking around. It was a long, rambling ranch house, a combination of wood and stone.

"It was originally the main house, Dad told me. The oldest part, there at the center, was built while Texas was still a republic. The gallery was once an open dog-trot"

"I can see it. The living and dining rooms would have been the original pens, right?"

"Probably. I will take your word for it. You know a lot about old architecture, according to Betsy Blake."

"Betsy put me on to the old historical district in Fredericksburg. That town has some history. It's a real friendly place."

"There was a time when it wasn't known for being so friendly. In fact, from the time of the Civil War until the beginning of the last century, it was almost a closed community. Most of the Germans there refused to speak English."

"Why was that?"

"They had been Union supporters, and the confederacy couldn't handle that. All through the war, and for a couple of years after, they were harassed, even lynched, by the partisan troops stationed at Fort Mason. Farms and ranches were burned, animals slaughtered, and people murdered in the streets. So the towns, especially the German settlements, just kind of pulled back from the rest of the state."

"Can't blame them. Weren't there local officials to stop it?"

"Some tried. In Sandy Creek, even, a sheriff was killed for trying to keep a couple of sixteen year-old boys from being hung."

"Shit. I hadn't heard that."

"Nobody talks about it much. I think most of the people who lived through it just wanted to forget. They did the best they could to rebuild, and tried to move on, but it wasn't always easy."

"It never is."

Khani could hear the grief in his voice. He had been working at moving on, but sometimes his memories just came back in a rush. "Sorry, Josh. That must have sounded insensitive."

"No. It's just me. Lately I've been forgetting, some of the time. When I remember, I still feel a little guilty for moving on."

"Give yourself time."

"Now you sound like Dan, and your old man."

"Dad likes you."

"I like him. He's got a pretty cool daughter. I think I'm beginning to like her, too."

"I am not a politician, Jack."

"You are an attorney, Daniel, and we need men who understand the law."

Daniel was surprised that the new provisional governor would take the time to travel all the way from Austin to talk to him, but Andrew Jackson Hamilton was a determined man.

"I have a law degree. I had my own personal reasons for earning one, but I've never practiced and don't plan to."

"I know your reasons, Daniel. I got to know your family pretty well while I was living in New Orleans, in exile, basically, during the war. I also know you were a Unionist yourself, and that you still hold to those ideals. The State of Texas needs your help."

"You have my help, and my sympathies, but even if I were willing to hold an office, I've got a ranch to rebuild."

"I get that. Hell, you weren't the only one who had to leave to stay alive, but the war is over, and there is much work to be done, and the secessionist Democrats are already working to regain power. If we can't build a stronger Republican Party in the state, we could be back where we started before the war."

"The federal government won't let that happen, Jack."

"Maybe, but if we don't handle this period of readjustment fairly, on our own, then Washington will have to take over, and it won't be pretty."

Daniel sighed at that, and said, "Jack, take a look around us here." The two of them had moved away from the main house and grounds, and away from the sounds of construction, so they could talk easily. Chase had, at Daniel's insistence, taken over the work on the additions to the house, and the work was well underway, but not yet complete. "I've got a full-size job here just getting my family resettled, and it's not just Maria and the children. Jake Holder's widow, her boys, and my mother-in-law are all part of it now. Until we get the expansion finished on the house, the women are stuck up at the old *hacienda* at Rancho Pineda. I couldn't leave them all here to go to Austin even if I wanted to. I know how serious your situation is. Like I said, I sympathize, and I will do all I can, from here, to support you, but it will have to be from here and Sandy Creek."

"I suppose I understand. I just hope you will be able to hang on to your land, and keep it going, especially if the radicals are successful in regaining control."

"We all do what we have to do, Jack," was all Daniel could tell his friend.

Chapter 15

"Give it a little time, Chase."

Daniel could see the young man was fuming.

"What the hell was it all for? Nothing's changed. The old guard is back in power. They managed to control the convention. They are doing everything they can to thwart Governor Hamilton's attempts to carry out President Johnson's plans. The Freedman's Bureau doesn't have the power it needs to be effective, especially now that the Democrats are back in office. They're passing labor laws that will likely turn into a new version of slavery."

In spite of the seriousness of the situation, Daniel had to hide a smile. Chase Holder was definitely his father's son. "That may not last long."

"How?"

"I got a letter the other day from my cousin in New Orleans. He says the same thing that Jack Hamilton has been saying, that Congress is refusing to seat the senators who skirted the amnesty regulations, including Hardin Runnels and the others who were elected from Texas and Louisiana. It looks like Congress is taking Reconstruction out of Johnson's hands. They are even trying to have him impeached."

"That might not be a bad thing."

"As a short term solution, maybe, but in the long haul, the elite power structure runs deep. The concept that it is okay for a handful of men to control the rest of the world, as wrong as it is, is a strong one. This group isn't going to just lie down and give up. They will just go further underground. We may be dealing with repercussions for a long time."

"In the meantime, Uncle, we've got beef to round up from both sides of the creek, and I'm wondering why we take the effort when we are still being blocked from taking them across the Red River by the Comanche."

"Most of the Penateka are settled on the reservations now, but some of them have joined the Quahadi and Quanah, their new chief. The Red River does seem to be the locus of their main camps, but we may not have to drive them that far."

"Mexico? Juan Cantina still has that route pretty well covered, doesn't he?"

"I haven't had any contact with Cortina since I left the valley.

Even then, he was taking a high cut of the profits. I was thinking more of Louisiana."

"Through the pine forests?"

"North of them. We could follow the Balcones Escarpment into the northern plains, and cross the river at Shreveport, like we did before the war."

"It would still be a long way to New Orleans, Uncle," but Chase was listening now. He had a great deal of respect for his father's friend, and was eager to listen.

"My cousin, Bill Thorne, has taken over the control of the family interests in New Orleans since my uncle died. He has some good ideas, himself, including setting up a market in Shreveport. He has even been building a second home there. He could serve three states from that city: Louisiana, Texas, and Arkansas."

"Sounds good."

"Only we would need to make the drive soon. Once Congress takes over Reconstruction, it won't matter that we were Union supporters when it comes to interstate commerce. The regulations, whatever the government decides to put in place, will apply to all southerners. We have a window, between now and then, when we could probably get it done. If we get it done fast enough, we stand to make a substantial profit, and the survival of the Double-R for the next few years after could depend on whether or not we succeed."

Chase agreed. His temper had cooled down and he was ready to listen.

"We are roughly about 400 miles from Shreveport," Daniel pointed out. "That's less than half the distance to the northern markets. Even if we don't try for more than fifteen miles a day, we could make it in just under a month, and we wouldn't hit the pine forests until the last day or so. My cousin Bill will be waiting for us by then, and will take over the cattle from there. We will need to leave soon, though, to get there before the winter snows. If we wait until next spring, there is a good chance that Congress will have taken Reconstruction out of Johnson's hands, and both Texas and Louisiana could be under military control. If we are going to make this work, we have to move the herd now."

"That shouldn't be a problem. We've had most of them bunched on the northern range since the round-up in the spring. There wouldn't be that much branding to finish. We shouldn't need more than a couple of weeks. We can do this, Daniel."

The older man smiled at that. He was no longer Chase's "uncle." He reached his hand out to his new friend and partner, and shook on their agreement.

"I don't like the looks of that sky."

"Norther? This early in the season?"

"Must be. It's not good. Diego?"

"It is close, *Padrone*. We should try to move the herd inside the *hacienda* walls. We would have some protection there, and it would be easier to keep them together."

Blue norther. It was a term Chase had heard from his early childhood, a name for the storms that would sweep down from the north without warning. Within less than an hour, they could engulf the hills with a deluge of rain, and the flood waters would begin at the highest point of the hills, and then race, with increasing force and speed, into the valleys below.

Diego continued, "If we can reach the *hacienda*, and draw the cattle inside its grounds, we might be able to hold them there until the storm subsides."

"And we would be holed up at the northernmost point of our property, and be ready to start the drive," Daniel added. "Chase, get the word out. We will meet inside the walls of the *hacienda* by nightfall."

The norther was a fierce one. Its winds and rains gathered strength as it moved southward. Toward the end of the day, the *vaqueros* were gathered, with most of the herd, inside the outer walls.

Daniel rode through the herd, trying to get an idea of how many head had been brought inside. He saw Diego, at length, and asked him, "Has anybody seen Dub and Adam?"

"They were seen near the foot of *Cabeza del Toro, Padrone*."

"Bulls-head Mountain?"

"Si, *Padrone*. There were many head that ran from the storm toward the mountain. Dub and Adam went after them."

Daniel was not pleased with the news. Bulls-head hardly qualified as a mountain, but it was the highest elevation around. The rain had been coming down hard there. The run-off would be coming down rapidly, with ever-increasing force.

By sunset, the rains had ended, but there was no word of either Dub or Adam. Neither Daniel nor Chase slept that night. They kept watch at the perimeter of the grounds, looking, and hoping, that they would see a glimpse of the missing pair. It didn't happen. At sunrise, a party went out to search for them. They found Adam's body first, tangled in a mesquite tree about half-way down the main ridge. It took longer to find Dub. He was almost buried in the mud at the foot of a draw.

As soon as Dub and Adam were buried, the men gathered to ride back to the *hacienda*, where Diego had stayed with the *vaqueros*, to make sure the cattle did not wander.

Daniel and Chase mounted grimly, and started to ride north, when they were joined by Maria and Molly, both on horseback, both wearing trousers and boots.

"Ma?"

"Maria, what do you think you are doing?"

"We do not think, *esposo*. Without our sons, you are two men short. We are taking their places."

"The hell you are!" The two men spoke in unison.

"Isabela and Lucia will look after Maggie until we return."

"No, Maria..."

"*Damn* this thing, Daniel!" He had never heard her call out with such force. "Do not argue with us. We are decided. Our sons will not die in vain."

Chase looked at his stepmother and saw the same determination in her face. He looked toward Daniel, and agreed when he heard him say simply, "Let's get moving."

They signaled Diego, and he and the *vaqueros* started driving the herd toward the northeast.

The days were monotonous, the work hard, but there were rivers all along the way, and no more early northers. Before long, they had left the escarpment and moved onto the plains, so the danger of another flood was behind them, but they still had to watch out for lightning storms that could spook the cattle and start a stampede. Maria was glad that there was not much time to think. They moved slowly, but kept going from dawn to dusk, and by the time they stopped, they were all too tired to do more than eat and sleep. Through the day, she would focus on her work, as did Daniel, and they had little to say to each other, but at night, he would pull her close, inside his blankets, and hold her tightly as they slept. First this job had to be finished; later they would have time for their grief. Her heart went out to Molly, who had to get through the nights alone. As they crossed the plains, the routine settled in, and the days went by quickly. She was surprised when they first saw the pine trees in the distance. The journey would soon be over.

And then it was over. They were sitting on the veranda of a comfortable raised cottage, the newly built home of Daniel's cousin Bill and his wife, Louisa. Maria and Molly had spent the afternoon soaking in steaming tubs, and both of them were now wearing borrowed tea dresses, loaned by Cousin Louisa, while Daniel sported a pair of dress trousers, a vest, and frock coat from Bill's wardrobe. Chase, once he had enjoyed a hot bath, had left to join Diego and the *vaqueros*.

Bill and Louisa had lost their oldest son during the siege at Vicksburg, and so, while their grief was less raw, they understood what their guests were going through.

"I would have liked very much to have known your son, Daniel, especially since he and I were both named for my father and your uncle."

"It is an honorable name, and he wore it proudly," Daniel replied, but he was not ready to talk about his son, and he knew that neither Maria nor Molly was ready either, so he shifted the conversation. "Our drive was successful, and mutually profitable, but, Cousin, what do you see as our prospects for the next few years?"

"It is too early to see clearly. I have concerns that the extremist perspective has not learned anything from these past years."

"I fear that as well. Odd, isn't it, that we chose opposite directions during the war, but for similar reasons."

"You are very well aware, Daniel, that the Thornes have never held with slavery. I think the difference in our choices has more to do with geography."

"Could you explain that, Cousin Bill?"

Louisa was a little taken aback that a woman would be so direct, and enter a conversation usually reserved for the men, but Daniel smiled at his wife's question, and looked to Bill for his answer.

"Your home, Maria, is on the frontier. Your situation is different from ours, here in the Deep South, especially in a major city like New Orleans. As a merchant, I find myself more in alignment with the industrial north, but, at the same time, my immediate customers are southerners, and for the most part, farmers, if on a very large scale. I was vocal in my stand for the Union before the war, but, once the decision for secession was made, my options narrowed drastically. In the end, I chose to stand with my neighbors. Our economy, here in the south, is too heavily based on agriculture for most of our people to see the situation from an industrial perspective. It is ironic, isn't it, when you think about it? My son died at Vicksburg at the same time as Thorne steamships were successfully maneuvering the Yankee Blockade." He shook his head. "There is no reason in war."

The trip home was much faster. Without having to worry about running the fat off their cattle, they made better time, and returned to the valley without incident. Once home, Daniel and Maria both hugged their daughter, and spent several days just listening to her talk about her adventures with *Abuelita* and *Tia Lucia*, as she had come to call the woman who had saved her life, as well as her mother's, on the day she was born.

But they had delayed their grieving too long already, so, as soon as they were certain that their daughter was doing as well as she could be, they left, on horseback, and rode northeast, losing any and every person who might have enough concern to follow them, and returned to the grotto, and from there to the hidden valley, and the stone house and its hidden caverns, to the cave with the massive red stone, and spent several days together in the healing light of the underground garden.

One afternoon, there, as they sat beside the rushing stream, after they had spent enough time there to feel strong enough to speak of what had happened, Maria asked Daniel some serious questions.

"I do not understand war, Daniel," she began, "but I can accept

141

that it is the result of human misunderstanding. And from that, I can find a way to accept Jake's death, and my father's. And I have been close to death, in the same way that Karin died, and I can grasp how the sacrament of birth, of such a great love, might make a mother's death acceptable, and her infant's death inevitable. What I do not understand is how, when the horrors of war were past, and we were finding our way back to a kind of order, at least, that God saw fit to take Dub and Adam. As hard as I try, and I am trying, I do not understand."

Daniel thought for a long while before he attempted an answer to a question he was not sure he completely understood himself. He knew that for his own sake, as well as for Maria's, he had to try. After a time, he started to speak, calling on the spirit of his grandmother to help him with his answer.

"This earth that we inhabit, and where we exist as guests, I think, has its own sense of order and law. We try to interpret that law, but we cannot completely understand it. But if you look closely, you can see that it has its own system of balance. A storm, whether it is a hurricane coming ashore, a snow storm, a strong wind at sea, a drought, or a late summer norther, with its rains and floods, is the way Nature strives to restore that balance. A cold dry winter might suck up the moist, warm air of the Gulf, or the south seas, creating a forceful enough whirling vortex to keep the warm air moving toward the cold north, so that it can reach to where it is badly needed. When that happens, most of the animals in its path will sense that it is coming, and do their best to get out of the way. Human beings, especially those of us who have had our understanding of Nature bred out of us, have the hardest time understanding her power and force, or her objectivity. Sometimes, we find ourselves standing in the way. She makes no promises to us, love, especially as individuals. Her intent is always about the greatest good for, I would say the greatest number, but that implies a countable objective, so let's just say she works for the good of the whole, and each of us, to that end, is an expendable part."

"Somehow, *querido*," Maria replied, "that begins to make some sense out of it all, but it doesn't lessen my grief."

"Nor mine." Daniel replied to her. "But what you and I have to help us through, is each other, at least for now."

Maria nodded, then added, "And Maggie, and Mama, and our memories."

They stayed with that, holding on to each other in silence, until

Maria finally said, "Daniel?"

"Yes, love?"

"Isn't it time to go home now?"

He stood, pulled her to her feet, and the two of them walked together, back to the stone house, gathered their gear, and rode back through the grotto and into their valley.